"Lucas, shouldn't we be looking for something?" Kyle asked softly.

She felt his hands touch her waist and, as her eyes grew used to the dark room, saw the glimmer of his smile.

"Later," he murmured.

She didn't want to keep him from his work again, but she couldn't help sliding her arms up around his neck. Strands of his thick hair slipped through her fingers like silk, and she caught her breath when he pulled her against him firmly.

"I thought you didn't want to rush things," she said unsteadily.

"I don't." He bent to press his lips against the bare flesh of her shoulder. "But I have to touch you, Kyle. I've spent so many nights . . . in the dark like this . . . remembering the softness of your skin. Remembering how your body felt against mine. Feeling your heart beating under my hand until it was my heart, and it was beating so hard that it hurt."

His low, compelling voice was a caress, flowing over all her senses until she could feel the words racing through her veins, tensing her muscles, weakening her bones. He pulled her close to him, and she felt an aching, yielding need of her own. She couldn't breathe, and yet her body had never felt so alive. . . .

WHAT ARE *LOVESWEPT* ROMANCES?

They are stories of true romance and touching emotion. We believe those two very important ingredients are constants in our highly sensual and very believable stories in the *LOVESWEPT* line. Our goal is to give you, the reader, stories of consistently high quality that may sometimes make you laugh, sometimes make you cry, but are always fresh and creative and contain many delightful surprises within their pages.

Most romance fans read an enormous number of books. Those they truly love, they keep. Others may be traded with friends and soon forgotten. We hope that each *LOVESWEPT* romance will be a treasure—a "keeper." We will always try to publish

LOVE STORIES YOU'LL NEVER FORGET
BY AUTHORS YOU'LL ALWAYS REMEMBER

The Editors

LOVESWEPT® • 231

Kay Hooper
The Fall of
Lucas Kendrick

BANTAM BOOKS
TORONTO • NEW YORK • LONDON • SYDNEY • AUCKLAND

THE FALL OF LUCAS KENDRICK

A Bantam Book / January 1988

LOVESWEPT® and the wave device are registered trademarks of Bantam Books, Inc. Registered in U.S. Patent and Trademark Office and elsewhere.

If you would be interested in receiving protective vinyl covers for your Loveswept books, please write to this address for information:

Loveswept
Bantam Books
P.O. Box 985
Hicksville, NY 11802

ISBN 0-553-21860-3

Published simultaneously in the United States and Canada

Bantam Books are published by Bantam Books, Inc. Its trademark, consisting of the words "Bantam Books" and the portrayal of a rooster, is Registered in U.S. Patent and Trademark Office and in other countries. Marca Registrada. Bantam Books, Inc., 666 Fifth Avenue, New York, New York 10103.

PRINTED IN THE UNITED STATES OF AMERICA

O   0 9 8 7 6 5 4 3 2 1

To my sister, Linda Lancaster,
who penned the verse

Prologue

He was a rotund little man, an unashamed paunch straining the seams of his tailored vest. Shiny wing-tipped shoes were on his small feet. He had a great leonine head with a cherub's face, small brightly twinkling eyes, and pouty lips. And he was so much a caricature of a strutting banty rooster pleased with his own importance that few people casually encountered would even look for more than that.

Lucas Kendrick was one of the few; he knew from past experience that the federal agent calling himself Hagen was about as harmless as a battleship and just as tough. So he stood in the dingy hotel room gazing out a dirty window for long moments before turning to cut off the droning voice of the federal honcho. "All right."

. Hagen blinked. "All right? Just like that?"

Lucas leaned back against the window frame and smiled sardonically. "There was really no need for all this cloak-and-dagger stuff," he said. "Meeting secretly like this. But you have to play your little games, don't you?"

"Mr. Kendrick, this is a serious matter," Hagen retorted in his best official manner. "And I felt it only fitting that you complete the job your friend Steele began a few weeks ago. The stolen artwork must be recovered and Rome prosecuted—"

"Sure he has them?"

"Positive."

Lucas didn't question the assurance. "Okay. So how do I get inside his estate? He has more security than we do."

The *we* Lucas used referred to Josh Long's worldwide financial empire, something that hardly needed clarifying between him and the federal man. Lucas was the chief investigator for Long Enterprises, and Hagen had spent the past year and more involving Josh and his men in various "assignments" for his agency.

The federal man looked somewhat searchingly at Lucas now, seemingly disturbed. "You're willing to accept the assignment, no questions asked?"

"Plenty of questions," Lucas corrected. "But why fight it? I'm the only one you haven't grabbed for one of your assignments; it was a matter of time. If I turn you down, you'll either talk me into it somehow, or you'll get me involved whether I like it or not. So how do I get onto Rome's estate?"

Hagen's cupid lips pursed slightly, but he responded readily enough. "Rome's having a weekend party soon; he does that from time to time, and his guest list is rather exclusive. There is a past . . . connection between you and the only single woman on that guest list. If she agrees, you'll be accepted onto the estate as her escort."

Lucas's expression never changed, but some tautness crept beneath his classical features, and his sharp blue eyes, flecked with gold, hardened. "Oh? Who is she?"

"Kyle Griffon." Hagen's small eyes were very wary.

Softly Lucas said, "What past connection are you talking about, Hagen?"

"We both know the answer to that, Mr. Kendrick."

"And just how the hell do *you* know? Her name was never in any of my reports."

"No, it wasn't. She was never linked to your undercover operation. You did an excellent job."

Lucas decided not to repeat his question. He really didn't want to know the answer. Instead he asked tersely, "What's the plan?"

More than an hour later Lucas again stood gazing through a dirty window. He was alone now, Hagen having left, and he looked back over his shoulder at the shoddy room. He had almost forgotten that secretive men met in dingy hotel rooms to discuss and plan dangerous operations.

Almost forgotten.

Ten years hadn't changed his memories, just made them more distant. He could still remember the cardboard taste of burgers and cold coffee, the stiffness of sitting for too long in cars, and the grinding frustration of political games having no place in his vision of the role of the law in human affairs.

He could remember undercover operations during which he literally had become someone else, and the disorientation of returning to the real world with memories of junkies and glittering life-styles and violence in the back of his mind. He could remember triumphs and tragedies, a little laughter and a lot of pain, and people briefly known.

He remembered Kyle Griffon.

Lucas half closed his eyes, shutting out the sight of a dingy, rainy street seen through a dirty window. And only sagging furniture marred by cigarette burns and too many hard years heard his low murmur.

"Oh, hell, Kyle, how am I going to face you?"

One

Lucas Kendrick's heart leapt into his throat. He rolled with that old but familiar feeling, annoyed that he still remembered how to ride an emotional bronc. It had been a long time. He clamped his teeth together and watched through narrowed eyes, telling himself he would have felt the same way while watching *anyone* with a death wish. It didn't help.

He hadn't really expected it to.

The triangular sail was about eighteen feet across and colored bright red and blue; dangling on a flimsy harness and steering the thing with a flimsy control bar was a small figure dressed in drab green.

Objectively speaking, he thought, it was a glorious sight. The hang glider banked and dipped and lifted as the strong mountain winds kept it aloft, its brilliant colors contrasting beautifully with the rich, varied, early-winter shades of green and brown in the valley and the distant snow-capped peaks of the Sierra Nevada Mountains. Lucas watched the glider, fists jammed into pockets and heart pounding in his throat, expecting a treacherous downdraft to snatch the flimsy craft and batter it to the valley floor far below. He couldn't take his eyes off it even long enough to fully appreciate a rare glimpse of a bighorn ram as it perched briefly on a rocky crag nearby and then vanished.

He knew the instant she spotted him, and he saw the glider bank in a tight turn and then hesitate for an instant before it began losing altitude in a long, sweeping descent toward him. He backed up automatically, giving her room, feeling himself tense even more. She cleared the edge of the cliff by inches, and her feet lightly touched ground.

She had to run only a few steps before she could stop the glider. The pointed nose of the thing tipped forward to rest on the ground, and she shrugged out of the harness, only then turning her head to study the visitor.

Without a noticeable expression, startling turquoise eyes scanned him from his windblown, silvery blond hair to his booted feet, taking in the backpack and rugged clothing he wore. Then casually she said, "Hello, Luc," and bent to collapse the hang glider and roll it up for carrying.

Well, what had he expected? Lucas wondered. He knew the answer, of course. Despite everything, *because* of everything, he'd expected a stronger reaction from her. Rather than a polite hello, he'd braced himself for something more along the lines of venom or hatred. Anger. Something.

And from any other woman that's what he would have gotten, even though it had been ten years.

At the very least, he decided with a little bitterness of his own, she might have asked why he'd come miles into the wilderness to find her—as it was patently obvious he had. And why he'd come now, after ten years. But not her.

Not Kyle Griffon.

She could trace her ancestry back hundreds of years, and even now the Celtic bone structure and dark coloring marked her indelibly as Welsh, no matter what other contributions had been made to her family's genetic pool. Her forefathers had been among the landed gentry back when such things counted, and five separate titles had graced her family name at various points in its history. And though her family hadn't arrived on American shores with the *Mayflower*, they'd probably been on the next boat.

Behind them they'd left their titles and land, and with them they'd brought generations of aristocratic breeding, shrewd intelligence, courage, utter composure, and all the family treasures they could hire people to carry. In the ensuing generations canny Griffons built various empires from those bits of silver and gold, glittering gems, and priceless paintings, and they hadn't looked back.

Lucas watched the slender figure in the drab green jumpsuit working expertly to bind up the glider into a compact bundle. He wondered if defying death was Kyle's way of dealing with her august lineage. In a family generally described as sober and businesslike, Kyle was a rebel and a rogue. Looking at her, it was easy to see that family traits had survived to bloom in her: She was enormously intelligent, composed no matter what the circumstances, innately proud without being arrogant, and courageous. Courageous, Lucas thought, sometimes to the point of insanity.

Unbidden, he also remembered the woman-child she had been all those years ago. Remembered her laughter and excitement, the spontaneous bursts of affection. Remembered a slender body locked to his own and blazing like a pure white flame, burning him. Searing away all doubt and uncertainty. At least for a while. At least while she touched him.

Lucas shook away the memories with an effort that was almost physical. But the heat of them lingered, teasing his mind with a ghostly touch and the fey sounds of quicksilver laughter.

He moved forward as she finished with the glider, and lifted the long bundle onto his own shoulder, saying only, "Let me." And his voice sounded normal, he thought.

Kyle didn't protest, but there was a faint glint of amusement in her blue-green eyes as she stepped back. "Just leave it by the porch, then," she directed, gesturing toward the snug log cabin a few yards away. She walked ahead of him, then paused on the steps until he'd set the bundle down. She held open the door of the cabin.

Lucas saw what he'd expected to see inside. It was modest but comfortable; all the modern conveniences but no luxuries. The overstuffed furniture stopped just short of being shabby, and colorful rugs dotted the shining wood floor. One big open room with a loft above for sleeping occupied most of the cabin, a kitchen divided from the main room by paneled walls, and a bathroom tucked away in back.

She could have built a castle.

He shrugged out of his backpack and left it by the door, still unsure of how far his welcome stretched. With Kyle, he reflected, it was difficult to be sure of anything. And he wondered then if he had imagined her feelings ten years before. Or had that seventeen-year-old girl greeted his departure just as she seemed to view life in general—with a shrug and a reckless smile?

No, he thought, not that. He had meant more to her than that, at least before he had left.

"Coffee's hot. Want some?"

"Please." He followed her to lean against the breakfast bar and watch her economical movements. And that hadn't changed, he thought; her grace hadn't changed, except to have matured somehow, become more fluid. The jumpsuit she wore showed him that the slender lines of a seventeen-year-old had become the fuller curves of a woman, and he tried to fight the knowledge that he wanted her now more than ever.

It was impossible, and he knew it was. There was too much between them, far too much, to allow them to return to being the people they once had been—even if both of them wanted to.

He watched her, aching inside.

She wore no makeup, and her thick sable hair was tousled, but she had spent too many years being carefully groomed in various expensive schools for her launching into moneyed society to be able to shed the peculiarly "finished" look instilled by the process. No matter what she wore or what she did, Kyle Griffon always would look aristocratic.

Pushing the thoughts away, Lucas accepted the

cup she held out and realized with a jolt that she remembered how he liked it. Sugar, no cream. She drank hers black. Disturbed by the realization that he wasn't alone in remembering, he followed her into the living area, watching her while she sank gracefully into an overstuffed chair, kicked off her light shoes, and curled up like a lazy cat.

"So. To what do I owe the honor of your presence on this sunny afternoon?" she asked.

Lucas sat down on the couch and looked at her, trying to see past those serene turquoise eyes. What was she thinking? Feeling? When he finally spoke, it wasn't in answer to her question. "When did you take up hang gliding?"

"When I got tired of skydiving."

He felt his teeth gritting again and fought to relax taut muscles. But his voice was nonetheless sharp. "And before that it was mountain climbing. And before that what? You were a stunt pilot, you raced cars in Europe, you went on some bloody dangerous safari in Africa and were nearly killed—"

One delicate brow rose, but there was no inflection of surprise in her casual voice. "You've been reading the supermarket rags."

He ignored that, mostly because it was true. "What is it with you, Kyle? A death wish?"

"A life wish, more like." She smiled a little.

Lucas felt another jolt. Her answer was just what he had replied years before when a friend asked why he risked his life as an undercover cop. But that was a long time ago. Now he was the chief investigator for a string of companies and corporations that spanned the globe. And there was a certain amount of danger in that from time to time. But he never risked his life recklessly. Kyle did.

She was still smiling. "You know, Luc, I've been wrong all these years. I thought when you walked out on me, you'd forget me in a week. But it seems you didn't. You've been feeling guilty, haven't you? Why? Did you think I'd developed some kind of complex, that I've been trying all these years to kill myself because of you?"

Lucas started to deny that but found he couldn't. It had crossed his mind more than once, because she'd gotten even wilder after . . . But by leaving her he had stopped at least one of her insanely reckless games. All he could manage to say, though, was, "You were very young."

She looked squarely at him, her serenely beautiful face unchanged by the passing of a decade. "Oh, I see. You were worried that you'd seduced an innocent kid." Something flickered briefly in her eyes and then was gone. "Want me to ease your conscience?"

"Dammit, Kyle!"

Her mouth twisted wryly. "Sorry. Low blow. I think I was entitled to that, though, don't you?"

After a taut pause he relaxed suddenly and smiled. It was over. *Past.* So play it her way, he thought. Play it light. Pretend it hadn't mattered. "You're entitled to more than that. What took you so long?"

"Ah. So you came up here expecting to be drawn and quartered? Not my style, I'm afraid. If I remember, I had a violent tantrum, cried for all of an hour, then called home and asked my father to have you killed." Her voice was light, dryly mocking, as if she hadn't cared.

"You've never had a tantrum in your life," he murmured.

"No," she agreed. "Mother wouldn't allow them. So undignified."

"I'm still alive," he offered, wondering if an irate father had asked Josh Long, "Is that why I should send her to Europe?"

"Hit men are expensive, especially to gratify wounded vanity."

Somewhat to his surprise Lucas found that old frustration could return as easily as all the other old feelings; beneath her flip response he could find nothing. What *had* she felt? "Kyle—"

"You don't want the truth, Luc," she said abruptly.

"Yes, I do." He was firm.

"Punishing me or yourself?"

He was surprised, rattled. Did she know what he had done for her? No. No, he had made certain she wouldn't know. There was only one thing she could know, and there was no hint of that knowledge in her face. "Why would I want to punish you?"

She didn't answer. "Look, it was ten years ago. We were different people then. Now, I know you didn't hike up the mountain just to rake up old memories after all this time. So why are you here?"

Given little choice in the matter, he reluctantly let it drop. For now. He pushed his own pain, his old feelings of confusion and uncertainty out of his mind and into the locked room where they had lived in darkness for ten years.

"I need your help, Kyle."

She looked mildly surprised. "Oh? With what?"

"There's a house—an estate, really—I need access to it socially. I need to be inside at least overnight, preferably for a weekend. It's Martin Rome's estate."

After a moment and in a completely expressionless voice she said, "Ten years ago I got involved with a young man who was supposedly a student at my college. Storybook stuff. I was swept right off my feet. And then he was gone. Really gone. According to the records, he never attended that college, and I could never find out anything at all about him. Now, ten years later, he appears in my life again and asks that I get him into the home of one of the wealthiest people in the country."

Lucas said nothing.

Kyle nodded, as though she'd expected silence. "So I have to wonder, Luc. I have to wonder why you want access to that home. And I have to wonder why in hell you think I'd help you to get it."

Lucas studied her, weighing the thought, wondering himself. Remembering a seventeen-year-old college freshman with a reckless smile; remembering a twenty-seven-year-old woman with a ten-year history of wildness hanging from a glider.

He wasn't reckless very often, but he decided then to take a chance. On her.

Lucas reached for his wallet and extracted a business card, handing it to her.

Kyle studied it for a moment, then looked at him. "Chief Investigator, Long Enterprises. Assuming I believe this, Luc, Joshua Long could get you into Rome's house just as easily as I could. So why won't he?"

He held her gaze steadily with his own. "He would. But it wouldn't do me any good. Because

Josh is known to have . . . interests in stopping criminal activities. Luckily, being an investigator keeps me out of the limelight; we've taken care that my name's never been linked publicly with the company or Josh. If he or any friend or employee of his were to approach Rome, there wouldn't be a scrap of evidence to be found."

"Evidence of what?"

"Illegally acquired artwork. Artwork bought from criminals for the price of a shipment of guns, also illegally acquired. We believe he has the art hidden—probably in a vault—somewhere in his house."

"We?"

Lucas hesitated.

Dryly she said, "I never knew who you were, Luc, and I certainly don't know you ten years later. So if you want my help, you'll have to tell me the whole story, or you might as well hike back down the mountain."

After a moment he nodded. "All right. I'm working temporarily for a government agency."

"Which one? FBI?" There was neither belief nor disbelief in her voice, only mild interest.

Lucas shook his head slightly. "No. This agency isn't listed in the Yellow or the White Pages. For all I know, it doesn't even have a name, official or otherwise. It's headed by a man who calls himself Hagen; that's probably not his real name. He spins webs like some damned poisonous spider—well, never mind. The point is, I'm working for him temporarily. I have to find that stolen art, or at least get enough evidence to indict Rome. And I have to go into his house socially; his estate employees are thoroughly screened."

"Wouldn't your background stand up to that?" she asked in an idle tone.

His blue gaze hardened, but he went on as if she hadn't spoken. After all, he could hardly blame her. "Normally Hagen would have a pristine background and impeccable references manufactured for a case like this, but there hasn't been time for it."

"Who came up with my name?"

"Hagen. He managed somehow to get hold of a guest list for a weekend bash Rome's throwing in two weeks. Your name was on it."

"Did he know you and I had . . . had met before?"

Lucas hesitated, then nodded. "He knew. I don't pretend to know how; Hagen doesn't give up his secrets or his methods. In any case, he picked you because of our past association and because you are the only single woman on the list. He figures you could bring a date without raising eyebrows."

"It would raise Martin's eyebrows," she said.

For an instant, a heartbeat, Lucas felt a dizzying sense of déjà vu. He was cold inside. It couldn't be happening again; she couldn't be involved in this. . . . He didn't want to have to make that kind of choice. Not again. Then the hard-won self-control of years kicked in, and he was calm. "You don't have an official connection with Rome," he said coolly. "No engagement, no attention by the press. An affair the society-press watchdogs haven't sniffed out?"

Kyle looked at him for a moment, expressionless, then said, "Nothing so definite. Let's just say that Martin doesn't give up easily, and has two strong beliefs. First, in the power of his own charms, and second in the reliability of erosion from water dropping on stone."

Lucas felt relieved and hoped it didn't show. "I

see. So he'd be surprised if you showed up with another man. But not terribly surprised?"

"A defensive move on my part, you mean? It's not my style, but he doesn't know that. He'd buy it if I turned up for his party with a buffer, I suppose."

They were silent for long moments, both sipping coffee, neither willing to ask or answer the flat question that had brought him up here to her mountain retreat.

Finally Kyle spoke. "It's a nice little story, Luc. Is that your real name, by the way?"

"Yes." He kept his voice even. "Lucas Kendrick."

She lifted an eyebrow briefly. "It was Lucas Kendall before, wasn't it? Well, never mind. A nice story. Lots of intrigue. Mysterious government agencies and agents, stolen art, wealthy criminals."

He had earned that disbelief, he supposed. "Look, do you trust Josh Long's word?"

"My father does. I've never met the man."

"Josh will vouch for me. And Hagen and the agency. I didn't want to involve him in this, but I don't seem to have a choice. Get in touch with him, Kyle, before you make a decision."

"I will." Her voice was flat with certainty; obviously she wasn't about to trust him blindly. Not this time.

Kyle stood by the window and stared out as moonlight painted the stark shapes of mountain scenery. It was dark in the loft, and she had moved with cat-footed softness to the window seat where she often sat. Lucas was sleeping on her couch and the cabin was silent.

She sat down on the cushioned seat and drew her legs up, hugging her knees as she looked out blindly.

Josh Long had vouched for Lucas instantly when she'd called, telling her with utter conviction that she could trust Luc and that he was indeed working for a man named Hagen who ran a secretive—and secret—government agency. He did have to get into Martin Rome's house, because the man was suspected of possessing stolen artwork purchased from criminals and paid for with illegal guns.

Kyle didn't doubt Long's word, and his faith in Lucas had been expressed too firmly to be in doubt, which left her with a great many disturbing questions.

Josh Long was no fool, and she knew from her father that he rarely erred in his judgment of men. Lucas had worked for him for "a number of years," and there was clear respect on both sides of that relationship. It was a vote of confidence that would instantly open doors in almost all social or business circles.

But it didn't—it couldn't—open Kyle's door.

She had closed down, put her feelings in a deep freeze, almost the moment she had looked down from her soaring glider and seen the sunlight glinting off his silvery hair. Even at that distance, his features indistinguishable, she had known it was he. And in that first flashing instant she also had known that she had been waiting for him to come back.

It shocked her.

For the first time in her life Kyle had cause to be thankful for a cold, distant mother who had taught her, if nothing else, to keep her emotions buried beneath a serene surface. Her mother would have been proud of her, she thought now with a pang of bitterness. When her feet had touched solid earth and she'd turned to Lucas, she had obeyed neither of the conflicting emotional reactions battling inside her.

She hadn't lashed out at him in bitterness, and she hadn't thrown herself into his arms.

Kyle closed her eyes and leaned her head against cool glass, allowing herself to remember, trying to understand what she felt now and what she had felt then.

Ten years ago he hadn't seemed much older than she, although he was supposed to have been a senior. She judged him to be in his mid to late thirties now, so she realized he had been older then than he'd pretended to be. Older and charming and heartbreakingly handsome with classical features and blue eyes that were more striking than any she'd ever seen. . . .

She opened her eyes after a moment and caught the silver chain at her throat with one finger, drawing the plain oval locket from its resting place between her breasts. A flick of her thumbnail opened the locket, and inside was revealed only a single polished stone. It was an opal she'd found in Australia five years ago. An opal that was blue with tiny flecks of yellow.

Like his eyes.

The moonlight streaming through the window picked out only the yellow flecks in the stone, causing them to gleam brilliantly but with no color, and Kyle absently rubbed the stone with her thumb before closing the locket and allowing it to slip back inside her silk pajama top.

Darkness and moonlight obscured colors, she thought. Time was supposed to obscure memories.

Ten years had changed him. He was broader across the shoulders, physically more powerful. His face was leaner, something under the surface of those classical features harder now, tougher. His voice was still low and curiously compelling, but there was, she thought, a shade of remoteness in it that hadn't been present a decade before.

Or maybe that was just when he talked to her.

What had he been then? she wondered now, as she had wondered since. And why had he pretended? Why had he masqueraded as a college student? And why, after a night of searing passion when she had given herself to him without reservation, had he vanished while she slept?

Without even leaving a note . . .

After the first agony had turned to numbness, Kyle had reached for any reason at all to excuse his behavior. He would have had a *reason*, she had decided, a good reason. And that had helped the hurt.

She wondered now, with the same shock as when she'd seen him this afternoon, if she had always really believed in the back of her mind and the deepest part of her heart that he would come back to her someday.

It was a strange shock, a frightening shock, and Kyle shook away the feeling for a second time. Ridiculous, of course.

She had been different then. Escaping to a large college from the cloying protection of her wealthy family, she had been wild with the reckless need to distance herself from the essentially cold, dignified, and unemotional aspects of her upbringing. All her emotions had been dammed by a wall of forced reserve, and when that wall had burst, she had nearly drowned in the floodwaters of release.

Did a woman ever really forget her first lover? Kyle knew only that she would never forget hers—because he was Lucas, and because he had been a part of that glorious period of freedom. She had loved him the way only a woman-child could love a man, with a reckless abandon that scorned possible hurt.

All her caged romanticism had burst forth in that long-ago flood during her first year of college. She had loaded her schedule with poetry and literature and history, and had memorized every great love poem history boasted. Madly idealistic, she had adopted one cause after another, throwing herself into each with boundless enthusiasm.

And she had fallen in love.

Now, from a distance of ten years, Kyle realized that loving Lucas had been a part of that freedom but not caused by it. She had been ripe for love, but what she had felt for him had not been born of mindless rebellion. It had never occurred to her then or since that he might not have won the approval of her family. She had given him all the pent-up affection and passions of her life, and he had responded. He had loved her in return. She had believed that.

Then.

She hadn't experienced that kind of freedom again. The skydiving, mountain climbing, hang gliding—none of it had been any more than a series of gestures. Outwardly reckless but with no burning fire of resentment and glorious release blazing behind it, she had been searching for something she could feel deeply about.

For the better part of ten years, she realized with a distant jolt, she had been going through the motions of rebellion and feeling . . . nothing. Except empty searching.

She could remember vividly the months of college and the weeks with Lucas. Remember feelings so vast, so powerful, that they had overwhelmed her.

And at the end the aching bewilderment of desertion that had, as the days turned into weeks, frozen her inside. With no explanation offered to her, she had made up various excuses for him, and that had kept a girl's love safely stored intact somewhere inside her. But he was gone; he had vanished from her life without leaving a trace. So she had obeyed her father's request a few weeks later and left college after a year, going to Europe and the finishing school her family thought proper. Years in limbo. And then a second rebellion, this one outward, while she'd remained frozen inside.

Kyle stared out at the peaceful mountains. Why? *Why?* If only she'd known what had been behind Lucas's actions then, perhaps, she could put it all in the past where it belonged. But she had never known, and even then the scope of his deception had bewildered her. He pretended he attended the university; he had a room on campus; he participated in activities. Why? What had been behind all that?

She had wanted desperately to ask him outright. She needed to know what had been more important to him than their feelings for each other. But it had been ten years, and somehow she couldn't bring herself to ask.

And now, knowing that he was working for a secret government agency, the questions became even more disturbing. Had he been doing something similar then? Both Lucas and Josh Long had made it clear that Lucas was working for Hagen only temporarily; this wasn't, apparently, the usual sort of job he undertook for Long Enterprises.

She had instinctively trusted Lucas ten years ago, and the results of that betrayal of trust had been devastating. Now he was back in her life, however briefly, asking for her trust again. Kyle felt more alive and aware than she had in too many years. But she was terribly afraid of trusting him. Afraid of allowing him back into her life. And that had nothing to do with Martin Rome and his alleged criminal activities.

She was afraid Luc would turn her life upside down again and then leave her, with no warning, to pick up the pieces alone. Again.

After she had talked to Josh Long, Lucas had asked for her decision, and she had stalled—there was no other word for it. The party was two weeks away, she'd said, and she wanted to think about it for a day or so. It had not been spelled out that he would remain here in her home until then, but both of them knew he would.

Feeling chilled, Kyle crept back to her bed. She knew why she had stalled. Because she needed time to work up the courage to face him with what had happened ten years ago. It wasn't possible to pretend to herself it didn't matter. She had to understand the series of events that had haunted her since then.

He had said he loved her, and in the morning he had been gone. She had to know why.

• • •

The faint sound of the shower woke her, and Kyle listened until she heard Lucas moving about downstairs in the kitchen. Then she rose and dressed, feeling edgy and tense. There was no conscious decision to confront him now, this morning, but when she went downstairs and into the kitchen, finding him leaning against the counter drinking coffee, the words emerged unbidden.

"Why did you leave me?"

And it seemed that he, too, was ready to talk, because he answered immediately.

"You know why."

"No. I don't. I've never known."

Lucas gave her a look of disbelief, something hard in his eyes, his jaw tense. "All right, maybe you didn't know why. Not completely. But you had to have a damned good idea when you found the suitcase missing. You had to know my leaving was connected to that."

Kyle shook her head slowly, confused. "Suitcase? What suitcase?"

"Oh, hell, Kyle—the heroin!"

Two

The suppressed violence of his rough outburst went through Kyle's body like an icy knife, leaving her numb. And his words made no sense at all.

"Heroin? Luc, what are you talking about?"

His eyes were hard, glittering, his face so wiped of feeling, it was like a mask. And when he answered, his voice was no longer violent but something far worse, because it was as empty as his face. "I'm talking about the suitcase stuffed full of white powder I found in your closet, Kyle."

Her mind was anesthetized; she could think of nothing but trivialities. "What were you doing in my closet?"

"Looking. Searching." His tone became clipped. "Trying to find evidence to clear you." He lifted his coffee cup in a jerky, mocking toast. "That's not what I found."

The gesture focused her scattered thoughts, and she moved automatically to find a cup. Coffee, cf course. This would all make sense when she'd had some coffee. She always needed coffee to wake up. She poured some and sipped, barely feeling the pain when she burned her tongue. Then she looked at Lucas and found that coffee didn't help at all.

She heard a stranger's voice emerge shakily. "Clear me of what?"

"Selling heroin to other students. Pushing."

"I didn't." Her denial sounded strangely weak and unemphatic to her own ears, just the way an innocent's denial always sounded when the accusation was one too wild and horrible even to contemplate.

"I *saw* you, Kyle." His voice was roughening, the words coming more rapidly. "I had photographs. A dozen times I watched while you met a supplier and exchanged money for drugs. I never saw you pushing, just buying, but you didn't use the stuff yourself and you were buying it weekly; you had to be pushing. Obviously for kicks, since you didn't need the money. And I saw you get the suitcase. I *saw* you. A week before. And that night, I had to know. So I looked for it while you were sleeping. And I found it."

Kyle's hand came out blindly and felt the solid comfort of an oak kitchen chair. She sat down automatically at the table and set her coffee cup before her trembling fingers dropped it. "No," she said numbly, shocked. "I never bought—or sold—drugs. Never."

"I saw you."

Belatedly her mind began to work. "You were a cop, weren't you?"

He met her unfocused gaze, his own eyes beginning to reflect a soul-deep uncertainty that had haunted him for a decade. Her shock and surprise were genuine; he could feel that. Then, what he had done . . . He pushed the thought away. "I was a cop. Undercover to find a campus link to a major dope dealer. The dealer was found dead a few days before—before I left."

"And you thought I was the link," she murmured.

"I *saw* you." The three stark words held the sound of something repeated so often and with such grinding force that they had been chiseled in stone.

Kyle remembered the suitcase now, remembered getting it; the incident had been so trivial, she hadn't thought of it since, or ever even missed the case. And she thought she understood. Drawing a deep breath, she said slowly, "You thought I was the link; you were sure of it. But I wasn't arrested or even questioned. Ever. Why not?"

He was silent, his gaze dropping to the cup in his hand.

"Why not, Luc?"

"You were seventeen," he said, still staring at his cup. "Wild, a little spoiled. Thoughtless. It was just a game to you, like all the other games. You didn't realize what you were doing. You didn't stop to realize it would have ruined the rest of your life."

She was staring at him. In a slow, wondering tone she asked, "What did you do?"

His mouth twisted in an unconscious, painful movement. He didn't want to tell her, but he had to. It seemed that this was the day to open up the past.

"Luc?"

"I was the only one who had proof, and I hadn't reported to anyone. I destroyed the photos and the heroin. There was a small-time pusher on campus, another student; he'd sold a little here and there to support his own habit. About the time you'd gotten the suitcase, he was found off campus, dead of an overdose. I reported to my superiors that as far as I could determine, he was the only one dealing on campus. I wasn't terribly popular with my superiors, and when I refused to answer questions about any of my findings, they decided I was hiding something. I would have resigned, anyway. They didn't give me the chance."

Kyle felt a jolt that took her breath away. "You . . . you were protecting me? You gave up your career to—"

"I was sick of the job," he said, interrupting flatly. "I'd already decided to quit and accept the position Josh had offered. I gave up nothing, Kyle."

She felt another jolt, this one far deeper and much more painful. She wouldn't have understood ten years before, she knew, because at seventeen there was no perception of such things. Lucas had indeed given up something to protect her, she thought, something far more important than a career.

He had given up his honor.

And it was only this realization that kept her from lashing out at him now for the terrible hurt inflicted on them both. For a fleeting instant she was tempted to let him go on believing that his sacrifice had gained something for someone, that he had indeed protected her from the results of insane folly, because she was afraid of what it would do to him to find out the truth. But he had to know.

No matter what it did to them, to each of them alone and to both of them, he had to know.

"Did you know I had a brother?" she asked suddenly. "He lived off campus until our father called him back home. That was just before you left."

Lucas frowned a little, thrown off stride by the seeming non sequitur. "I knew. He was killed a few months after you went to Europe, wasn't he? A car crash?"

"Amazing what money can do." Her voice was quiet and flat. "A car didn't kill my brother."

"Then what did?"

"Heroin. He died of an overdose."

Lucas began to feel curiously chilled inside. A cop's training took over, sifting through new facts and old ones. A brother who used heroin and died from it—and who had lived in an apartment near the university campus where his younger sister attended classes. A sister who was wild and a little spoiled but didn't use drugs . . .

Kyle kept her eyes fixed on his face, and her voice was soft. "I adored him. You said I was a little spoiled; Dorian was a lot spoiled. Our father instilled in him all the beliefs of the family, but Dorian twisted them to suit himself. He thought that wealth and power meant everything. Ultimately he believed he was invincible. And since he was the heir, he was indulged. He never would admit to a fault when we were kids; if something happened—a rock breaking a window, or a vase shattering—he always blamed me. And I took the blame because I adored him and it seemed right that I take his punishment for him."

She sighed softly. "I was blind. The packages, the suitcase, they were his. I was used to doing things for him, without question. And since I was . . . well, rather involved with what was happening in my own life then, I wasn't much interested in what all the *favors* really were. I never looked in the packages, the suitcase. Maybe if I had—"

If I had, he might still be alive. If I had, I would have confided in you, and ten years of our lives would have been different.

Lucas set his cup on the counter and walked out of the kitchen. Kyle didn't turn, but she heard the front door open and shut quietly. She closed her eyes, and in the silence of the house her voice sounded as though it were wrenched from the depths of her body.

"If I had, you wouldn't have sold your honor for me."

Kyle was a realist; she knew it hadn't been completely her fault. She had been young, thoughtless, and in love. Too preoccupied with the damburst of her own feelings to notice that Lucas had grown quieter those last couple of weeks. Too self-involved to understand why she'd sometimes caught him looking at her with a brooding expression. Too accustomed to doing things for her brother to notice anything unusual about the packages she picked up for him.

And Lucas . . . Considering what he had sacrificed for her, he clearly had been in love with her. He hadn't lied about that. But even though he had been an undercover cop, what had happened to them was also his fault. Trust was a part of love; he should have doubted the evidence at least enough to confront her with it.

But Lucas hadn't loved enough, or doubted enough. And she had loved her brother too blindly to question. And because of that, each of them bore a wound that was raw and bleeding. Her wound was less, she thought, because knowing what Lucas had done for her would start the healing now. *He hadn't left her lightly.* But Lucas . . . His wound was a deep and terrible one, damaging an integral part of his very self.

She had the comfort of knowing he had not loved or left her lightly, that he had sacrificed something of himself for her. But Lucas had the devastating awareness that he had sold his soul for nothing.

If ten years hadn't separated them, Kyle would have gone out then in search of him, all her instincts telling her that a man shouldn't be alone while facing such a terrible truth. She had earned the right to go after him all those years ago in a single night of passionate giving.

She wanted to go after him, even if her comfort could be no more than presence or a simple touch. But she couldn't. What he had done for her had changed him in ways she might never fully understand, had made him less than he was—and more than he was.

Far back in a dark corner of her mind was another reason she couldn't go after him now. Love was perhaps the strongest human emotion of all—and also the most fragile. And it was less likely to die a quiet death than to alter itself to bitterness and regret. Sacrifice always cost someone something. Lucas might have learned to hate her in ten years.

He might have learned to hate her in ten minutes.

Kyle got up slowly and went into the living room. She sat on the couch and picked up the phone, dialing a number even more familiar than her own. Her father was an early riser, and the household staff as well, but even the butler sounded sleepy when he answered.

While she waited for her father to come to the phone, Kyle fretted about the phrasing of her question. There had been little between her and her father; Dorian had been the pride of his life. To her, Phillip Griffon had always been a strict authority figure, and what she felt for him was made up more of respect than affection. A calm, humorless man who sat at the head of both boardroom and dining tables, he had made no secret of his disapproval of her, his disappointment in her.

She had never learned how to talk to him.

"Kyle?" His voice was as dry and precise as always, as unhurried and without much inflection.

"Hello, Father." There was no need, she knew, to ask how he and her mother were; he would consider that a waste of time. She stared fixedly at her fireplace and tried to find the words. "I—I need to ask you about something."

"What is it?"

"It's about Dorian."

There was a long silence, and then his voice came through the lines flatly. "Your brother's dead."

Kyle half closed her eyes. "Yes. Did you know he was using drugs while I was at the university?" Like all hard questions, hers came out quickly, bluntly, and without tact, as she had been afraid it would.

"I won't allow his name to be dirtied," Phillip Griffon said. "Has some scandal sheet approached you, Kyle? Your family name is important, even if you don't think so."

She felt cold and lonely. "Nothing like that, Father. I just need to know. It's been ten years— don't you think I have the right to know? *Was* he using drugs then? Is that why you called him home?"

"Kyle—"

"Father," she said evenly, "I've just found out that I was almost arrested because of what Dorian was doing. I have the right to know."

"Just found out?" His voice sharpened. "From whom?"

"An ex-policeman. I want to know if you knew about Dorian's life then. Did you?"

"Who is this ex-policeman? What has he told you about your brother?"

"Will you answer me, please?" She felt like screaming at him but didn't, of course. "Did you know before you called him home that Dorian was using drugs? Selling them?"

"I suspected," he said finally, briefly.

She was looking blindly at nothing. "I see. Why did you send me to Europe? Did you suspect me too?"

Again he hesitated. "No harm in telling you now, I suppose: I was warned that drugs were common on campus and that it wasn't a safe place for a sheltered seventeen-year-old."

She felt detached. "Who warned you?"

"Joshua Long. It seems he had a friend on campus who warned him about the problem."

Meaning Lucas, she knew. What had it cost his pride, she wondered, to turn to his new employer and request a favor such as that one?

"Who is this ex-policeman?" her father asked sharply.

"Never mind."

"Really, Kyle, have you no thought of your family's name or my position? If this man has information potentially damaging to us, I must be made aware—"

In a still, remote voice she said, "Oh, don't worry, Father. He doesn't need to sell information to the scandal sheets. And blackmail isn't his style. He won't disturb the precious family name." And she quietly cradled the receiver.

Her father didn't call back. But then, she hadn't expected him to.

Suspected. Her father had suspected that the apple of his eye was using and selling drugs. So he had yanked him back home, so quickly that Dorian hadn't been able to reclaim the suitcase full of his latest purchase. Knowing Dorian, he had shrugged off the loss of those drugs, quickly found a supplier closer to home, and never even thought to warn his sister to drop that damning suitcase into a river.

And three months later he was dead.

Kyle was beyond assigning blame to anyone for any part of that tragic series of events. It was over, ten years over, and they all had to learn to live with the results.

Her father had learned to live with whatever he

felt by never mentioning his dead son by name and by acting as if he had no offspring; from her years in Europe on, Phillip Griffon had taken no further interest in Kyle. And her mother coldly blamed Kyle for the loss of Dorian. She should have been able to do something; after all, hadn't she always watched out for her brother, even if he was two years older?

But what of the other two who had suffered— Kyle and Lucas?

She didn't know, not really. Not now. Not yet.

Hours passed before Lucas came back into the cabin. Kyle was on the couch, curled up before a blazing fire drinking coffee. She didn't look at him, just told him that coffee was in the kitchen. He was probably chilled to the bone, she thought, because it had suddenly turned cold outside, the way it sometimes did in the mountains. The radio was playing softly, and the weather forecast had just been announced. Snow within twenty-four hours.

She heard him go into the kitchen where faint sounds indicated he was ready for some kind of warmth, at least. In a little while she felt him sit on the couch a foot or so away from her. Still, she didn't look at him.

Softly, wary of disturbing the high wire under her feet, she asked, "Do you have a family?"

"No." He didn't elaborate.

"Have you ever been close to anyone?"

"A few friends. You."

It surprised her so much that she turned her head to look at him and found his gaze steady on her face as he sat half turned toward her. And she was even more surprised when he went on in a quiet, musing tone.

"I think I went a little mad when I met you. You were . . . someone very special. You were at a crossroads in your life, suspended between woman and child. I don't know, maybe if I'd had sisters and watched them grow, you wouldn't have affected me quite so strongly. I think that was a part of it, watching you turn into a woman before my eyes. And you were—forgive me—starved for affection."

Kyle nodded slowly, unable to take her eyes off a face that had grown worn and haggard these last hours but was still incredibly beautiful and no longer a mask. And with all he must be feeling himself, he still thought of *her* feelings. She swallowed hard. "I guess I was."

"Me too." He smiled just a little, but then the smile died and there was something bleak in his vivid eyes. "I was nine years older than you; I'd been a cop for five years. And when you work undercover, you—there's a danger of losing yourself. But I forgot all that when you were with me. You were so untouched. So damned innocent of cruelty. You were just waking up to life. There were no shadows in you, no nightmares in your memories. You jumped on every bandwagon that passed, just for the joy of the ride."

"And you believed selling heroin was another bandwagon." She hadn't meant to say it, realizing only then that there was a wound because he hadn't trusted her enough.

"No." His response seemed to come from deep inside him, where there was no question. But then he shook his head. "I don't know. It's haunted me because I could never be *sure*. I had never faced you with it."

"And now? Looking back?" She gazed at him steadily. "Why did you do it, Luc? Because you thought you loved me?"

"Because I knew you loved me. Or loved what you thought I was." His voice was low, tentative, as if it were a recent discovery. He looked down at the cooling coffee in his cup. "You looked at me like I was a god, Kyle, did you know that? Like I'd just stepped down off Olympus. And that's heady stuff. Seductive stuff. I'd spent months at a time rubbing elbows with the scum of the earth, and sometimes all that dirt weighed me down. But I had to be worth something, because Kyle looked at me like that.

"But *I* knew I had feet of clay." He looked at her then, with a crooked smile and a sheen in his eyes. "And I think I was less afraid of being disappointed in you than of having you be disillusioned by me. You thought I was special, and I didn't want to have to tell you I wasn't. That I was just a cop trying to do a dirty job. That I was watching you and following you to do that dirty job."

Kyle stared at him. "So it didn't matter whether I'd done what you suspected? It just mattered that I not find out you weren't what I thought you were?" She felt bewildered, felt somehow hurt and . . . cheated. "Luc, girls grow up. And they find out that men aren't gods. Even the ones they think they love."

"I know." He half closed his eyes. "Kyle, I can't

give you a clear list of reasons why I did what I did. It was a jumble then. And now. I was feeling too much to sort one thing from another. And since then I've felt a lot of bitterness because I turned my back on my responsibilities and walked away from my job."

"And me? What did you feel about turning your back on me, Luc? How did you feel leaving my room and knowing I'd wake up alone, my one-night lover vanished without a word? Did you even consider just how brutally I found out about gods with feet of clay?"

He almost flinched from the sudden bitterness in her voice. "Yesterday," he murmured, "I felt frustrated because I didn't know what you were thinking or feeling."

Kyle tried to reclaim her surface calm but found it gone, out of reach. "Yesterday *I* didn't know what I was thinking or feeling," she said tightly. "And this morning I felt shattered because I thought you'd sold your pride, or your honor, or something, to protect me. And now I'm just plain *mad*, because what you did was for all the wrong reasons!"

Lucas was gazing at her with an odd, searching look, and he made a rough sound that might have been a laugh. "When did I stop being godlike, Kyle? Ten years ago when you woke up alone? Or ten minutes ago when I admitted I made some human mistakes? What hurts worse—that I left without a word or that I left for purely selfish reasons?"

She felt a shock that was almost physical, a painful jolt that knocked anger and disillusion-ment completely aside. "No. I—"

"I suppose we all do that," he said quietly. "Rationalize to protect our self-images. Ten years ago I told myself I was protecting you, I was doing something noble, when all the time what I was trying to protect was your very attractive image of myself. I couldn't tell you who I was without shattering that image. So I walked away. And what did I leave you with? Your own rationalizing."

It was true and she knew it. And because he was being so painfully honest, she could be no less.

"It was a mystery," she said slowly. "No record of you at the university. No one who knew where you'd gone. A mystery. Strange. And I built on it. I told myself over and over that you wouldn't have left without a word unless you had a strong reason. I imagined wild things."

He didn't ask her to elaborate, saying, "And this morning you suddenly had a reason. I left to protect you, sacrificing—what was it you said?—my honor or my soul in the process? I wasn't the only one who painted myself noble."

Kyle nodded, surprisingly unembarrassed, but said after a moment, "I think you did sacrifice something, though."

"I did," he agreed immediately, wryly. "I sacrificed whatever may have evolved between us. And perhaps I gave up a part of my—oh, honor, for want of a better word. I turned my back on the responsibilities of my job. But it felt like an even trade then. That part of me for your image of me."

She felt as if she were looking at him for the first time, a stranger met while rounding a sudden corner. "We never knew each other at all, did we?" she asked wonderingly. "You knew a kid trying too hard to be a woman, and I knew an image in my mind."

He smiled another twisted smile. "It's taken me these ten years to see myself clearly," he said. "And the last of that noble image shattered when you told me I left for nothing. What about you?"

"I don't know. I think I'm just beginning to see myself." She was silent for a moment and then, jerkily, she asked, "Did you plan that last night?"

"No." Then he swore softly. "I don't know. I knew you were untouched. That's an old-fashioned word, but it fit you. Maybe I wanted that. You said it yourself. Girls become women and find out that men aren't gods. I think I wanted to make love to you before you found out."

Slowly, quietly, the last lingering remnants of that godlike image faded away. He had fallen off the pedestal she had put him on all those years ago, and she didn't know what he was now. And Lucas seemed to read her mind—or the expression on her face.

"I'm just a man, Kyle," he said quietly. "I've made more mistakes in my life than I like to think about, but I hope I've learned from most of them. What I did to you was cruel, and if I could go back and change it, I would. But I can't."

Kyle stared into the fire, feeling cold and painfully aware of a tearing grief. He hadn't been *real*. She had given herself, everything she was, to a man she had made up in her own mind. And ten years couldn't soften that blow. Ten years had made it worse, because that image had lived in her mind so long, it had seemed even more real.

And now he'd torn it out by the roots, and the bare spot hurt terribly.

"I'm sorry," he said quietly.

"It doesn't help," she snapped.

"I know."

She looked at him then with burning eyes. "You should have stayed away."

"So you could go on loving a god?" he asked bleakly.

"It didn't hurt, not like this. At least there was no one to tell me that you weren't real."

Lucas shook his head. "But I *was* real, dammit. I am real. Kyle, I needed that image of yours then, because there was so much dirt in my life and I was *tired* of it. Call me a bastard, a heel—anything you want. I deserve it. But I didn't deliberately set out to hurt you. I never wanted that."

He looked at her with restless eyes. "Sometimes through the years I wanted to see you so badly, I ached. I looked for your name in the magazines and newspapers, and some of the things you were doing scared the hell out of me." He hesitated, then said, "There was never any hint of a man in your life, though."

She knew what he was asking, and her smile was bitter. "What man could live up to the memory of a god?"

"Kyle—"

"I know. You're sorry."

His smile was bitter too. "You forgave me for leaving you, Kyle. Ten years ago. You just can't forgive me now for being human."

He rose and carried his cold coffee to the kitchen, then returned to gaze down at her with no expression. "I'll tell Hagen we'll have to find another way into Rome's house."

Kyle had forgotten about that. She looked up at Lucas and felt a sudden, searing anger. "Just like that? So for a second time you're going to waltz through my life, drop a couple of bombshells, and then simply leave?"

"What the hell do you want me to do?" he demanded, sliding his hands into the pockets of his jeans, his face tightening. "We're strangers, Kyle. And once upon a time this stranger hurt you. What do you want, atonement? There's nothing I can do to change what happened. I can't even *try*, because you won't forgive me for being human."

Kyle automatically set her cup aside and stood up, facing him. And she didn't know what she would say until the words emerged. "I want to know what I missed, Luc. I'm a woman now, and we both know I don't believe men are gods anymore. I think I deserve to know who really walked away from me ten years ago."

Lucas gazed at the lovely face that wasn't serene anymore; ten years hadn't aged or changed her surface tranquillity, but the shattering of illusions had. She looked older than yesterday, the new maturity making her more beautiful than ever. And he had a sudden premonition that this time it would be he who would be left hurting and alone.

"So, I don't walk out that door?" he asked steadily enough.

"I don't know. Do you? It's two weeks until Martin's little weekend party. Is that long enough for two strangers to get to know each other?"

"What have you got in mind?" He was trying not to remember a slender body flaming with awakened passion. Trying not to remember how badly he had hurt himself by leaving her and how long he had hurt. She probably wouldn't believe him. Probably wouldn't believe he still woke sometimes reaching out for her.

Kyle shrugged. "I don't know. I think I want . . . I want time to heal. I trusted you then, and I haven't trusted anyone since. No other man could ever measure up to what I thought you were. Even though part of me kept you on your pedestal, another part of me never wanted to be hurt like that again. So I just stopped feeling. I want to feel again, Luc."

His smile was forced, stiff. "Hate me. That's feeling."

"I don't want to hate you." She looked at him searchingly, wondering what she did want.

He wondered too. "Then what? Just two nice grown-up, adult people on a two-week date? To see if we click?"

"Maybe we would," she said soberly.

Lucas walked over to the window because he had to move, had to stop looking at her. He looked outside instead. "And if we did?"

She didn't know. Did she want to take such a risk? A god, with all his thunderbolts, couldn't hurt a girl the way a man could hurt a woman. Kyle felt confused, afraid. "I don't know," she said finally, almost inaudibly. "Do you?" She watched his shoulders square, as if he were bracing against something.

"I left you once," he said, very low. "Tell me to

go and I'll leave you now. Later I may not be able to leave you, Kyle."

"Why not?" She was suddenly tense, aware that a great deal depended on his answer.

He turned to face her, leaning back against the window frame. He looked as drained as she felt. "If I stay, we'll very probably end up being lovers. I hope you know it."

She hesitated, then nodded slowly. A day for honesty, indeed. "I know. It's possible."

"Are you willing for it to happen?" His voice was terse, controlled.

Kyle met his gaze steadily. "You wanted to make love to a girl who didn't know the difference between men and gods; maybe I want the possibility of making love to a man knowing the difference."

"You may not want the man I am."

"I want to find out if I do."

"While I wait patiently?"

"While you find out if you want a woman who's no longer a girl, Luc. I'm not her anymore. You may not want me now."

"I do."

She blinked, felt a sudden heat course through her body. "You do?"

On a sigh he said, "Kyle, I never stopped wanting you."

Dropping bombshells, she thought. He was good at that. "How can you know? You don't know *me*."

"It doesn't matter. I knew how I felt yesterday when I watched you soaring around out there hanging under that glider. I was scared to death you'd fall. Just like I've been scared all these years every time I saw a picture of you or read an article about you. Scared you'd wreck the damned race car, or get hurt or killed jumping out of a plane or climbing a mountain."

Kyle realized then that her arms were crossed over her breasts, that she had been trying unconsciously to hold him off, close him out, stop what he was saying. Because with her illusion of him gone, it was *hard* to believe what he was telling her. Hard for a woman to grasp that a girl's dreams of a god were shallow and insignificant when compared to a man's emotions that had lasted ten long years.

She had stored her dream in a deep freeze, but it seemed Lucas had lived with his.

Ignoring the body language that he understood fully, Lucas said softly, "And that's why I couldn't leave you later, Kyle. I never said good-bye to you, so I never really lost you. If we were lovers and you wanted me to go, I'd have to say good-bye, because I could never leave you the way I did before. I'd have to say good-bye and lose you completely, and that's something I just don't think I could do."

Kyle couldn't seem to breathe very well and she was shaking inside. "You make it sound so important," she whispered. "So terribly important."

Lucas pushed himself away from the window slowly and crossed the room to stand before her. His hands slid from his pockets and lifted to hold her shoulders carefully—too carefully. "It is important," he murmured, and bent his head until his lips touched hers.

He didn't kiss her like a stranger. A flood of memory rushed through her mind and triggered a storm of sensations, memory of hot, possessive kisses and hands that had made her body his own, imprinting her with the very essence of himself. And her body, attuned to his as instantly as it had been so long ago, swayed toward him.

She was aware of rough flannel and hard muscles under her fingers as her hands slipped around his lean waist and moved slowly up his back. Her heart smothered her with its pounding, and strength flowed from her limbs as if something inside her, some barrier, had ruptured, given way. The slow, stark possession of his tongue ignited a curl of fire deep inside her where no fire had burned for a decade, and she barely heard the faint, hungry sound that tangled in the back of her throat.

As her body moved to be closer, his hands slipped down her back in a lingering caress that left a trail of stinging awareness. It had been like that before, she remembered dimly; he had always made her more aware of her body, her senses. He had always been able to bring her alive with no more than a look or a touch. Her body remembered. . . .

But the touch of his body felt slightly different, she realized. He was harder, stronger. His kisses were rougher, more demanding, his desire more direct. She was different, too, but neither of their differences changed her reaction to his passion. Her breasts were fuller, her hips more rounded in the womanly figure gained by years, but she remembered. And all her senses, frozen for so long, recalled only too vividly sensations known but briefly.

Nothing else mattered. Not ten years, or old and new hurts, or illusions shattered. She didn't know this man, but her body knew him, wanted him, and willpower was a frail thing overpowered by sheer, burning need.

Lucas tore his mouth from hers with a hoarse sound, and his hands dropped to pull her hips fiercely against his lower body. "It *is* important," he said thickly. "I haven't felt like this for ten years, Kyle. And I've learned too much since then to throw it away without a hell of a fight."

Three

Kyle tried to get hold of herself, but it was difficult when she was so aware of his arousal and her own. She wanted to back away, put some distance between them, but her body refused to allow that escape. So she rested her forehead against his shoulder and tried to think. She was so tired and drained, and she wanted him so badly.

But then she thought of everything that had happened between them, and strength returned. There was a slow, grim anger inside her, a resentment at how he had cheated her, how she had cheated herself. She backed away from him abruptly until they stood apart, and looked at him with her chin lifted.

"I'm not a girl anymore, Luc. And I won't fall into bed with a stranger this time."

"Kyle—"

"I mean it! Because it isn't that easy. Being

lovers isn't an automatic step for us; it may never happen."

"It'll happen," he said roughly. "Don't try to tell me I imagined your response, Kyle. *I'm* the one who stopped, not you. We wouldn't have made it to the bedroom!"

Her voice emerged soft and firm, and there was more emotion in that quietness than Lucas would have thought possible.

"I gave you everything ten years ago. No matter what I thought you were, I gave you everything I was. And you gave me *nothing*, Luc. Not even honesty. I won't let that happen again. I want to find out who you are, and who you were, and *then* I'll decide if I want you to have who *I* am."

After a moment Lucas nodded. She had the right. And he knew he was willing to gamble on something he hadn't dared to ten years ago. He was willing to gamble that Kyle could learn to love him with the intensity that she had loved that image in her mind.

"I love you," he said, and he was startled because the words had emerged totally against his will.

Kyle looked at him, a curious, searching look. She didn't know if she believed him. But whether she did or not, she felt—nothing. "I don't seem able to feel much of anything about you right now," she said slowly.

"You want me." His voice was tight.

"Maybe I want the only thing left of that image." Kyle shrugged suddenly. "I don't know. But I mean to find out, Luc. If you stay."

"I'm staying." He drew a deep breath. "I don't seem to have much choice."

• • •

They were strangers, strangers with a past and a strong awareness of physical desire. They were cautious, tentative, both wary of moving too fast. And they were very careful to avoid touching. But they were able to find a neutral ground, and both clung to that prosaic space.

They fixed a late lunch in the kitchen, avoiding getting in each other's way and being almost painfully polite. They ate, making bland conversation about the weather. They cleaned up after the meal with studied casualness.

This state of affairs might have lasted indefinitely—or might have blown up in their faces. However, a distraction presented itself. Actually two distractions, making a suitably dramatic entrance.

Kyle, more attuned to the sounds of her home than Lucas, heard it first and went out to stand on the front porch. He went with her, hearing what she'd heard as soon as they were outside in the crisp air.

"Helicopter."

She looked at him. "I'm not expecting company. How about you?"

"No." But he was frowning, and when a sleek white craft set down yards from the cabin, he wasn't surprised to see the logo etched in blue.

"Long Enterprises," Kyle said, sending him another glance.

Lucas slid his hands into his pockets and said nothing, watching while the helicopter lost power and the thumping rotors slowed to silence. Two men climbed out of the craft and approached the cabin briskly.

Kyle watched curiously as they neared, one slightly ahead of the other. The first man was rather large and clearly powerful, his lean face open, almost ingenuous, unremarkable but curiously pleasant. His hair was a rusty shade of brown and his eyes somewhere between blue and gray. The second man was tall and leaner than his companion, with copper hair and light brown eyes. His face was humorous, his smile somewhat lazy—but he moved with a kind of wired tautness that spoke of an incredible amount of energy.

As the first man reached them he said, "Wow!" rather inelegantly as his gaze swept over Kyle, then he addressed Lucas. "No wonder you didn't report in."

Sighing a little but looking annoyed and somewhat impatient, Lucas murmured, "Kyle, this is Kelsey—better known as Hagen's right arm."

"I am not," Kelsey instantly denied, offended. "Snakes don't have arms. I just slither along beside him sometimes," he confided to Kyle.

"How do you do?" she murmured gravely.

Just as grave, he replied, "I'm not really sure. I think I win about half the time."

Kyle found herself smiling and wasn't surprised.

"And this other character," Lucas said, "is Rafferty Lewis. He's Josh's attorney, and I don't know what the hell he's doing here."

"I flew the bird," Rafferty said, as if that explained everything. He smiled at Kyle. "Hello."

"Hi." She glanced at Lucas, noting his somewhat mutinous expression, then back at the visitors. "Why don't you gentlemen come inside?"

Kelsey looked at Rafferty. "You see? I told you I

was a gentleman, but no, you wouldn't believe me. Kyle is obviously a woman of great perception."

"She doesn't know you yet," Rafferty chided.

"I want to know what the hell you're both doing here," Lucas said as they went inside the cabin, effectively cutting short the discussion of Kelsey's personality.

"Hagen," Kelsey said.

"Josh," Rafferty said at the same time.

They looked at each other and scowled.

Kyle tried not to giggle as she sat in a rocking chair by the fireplace. She remained silent, mostly because she was relieved by the interruption these men presented, but also because they were clearly friends of Luc's and would therefore give her an opportunity to learn a little more about him. Or at least she hoped so.

"Let's have it," Lucas demanded.

Kelsey made an "after you, Alphonse" gesture to Rafferty and then sat down on the couch, looking innocent.

Rafferty used a shoulder to prop up the fireplace across from Kyle and smiled. "Nothing earth-shaking," he told Lucas placatingly. "When Kelsey asked for a ride, Josh just thought I should come along and hear what he had to say."

Lucas looked at Kelsey. "You mean you had the nerve to ask Josh to lend you a chopper and pilot?"

"Hagen had the nerve," Kelsey explained, somewhat indignant. "Said he was on a tight budget. Come on, Luc, you know he has the nerve of a burglar. And Josh could have said no. If you people would just *say* no a few times, Hagen might leave you alone." He mused silently, then said in a wistful tone, "I hope I'm around to hear it, though."

"Where's the boss?" Lucas asked Rafferty.

"New York." The lawyer shrugged. "He's tied up with that merger. Jed's handling it. My partner," he explained to Kyle, who nodded. Rafferty looked back at Lucas. "Raven and Sarah are trying to find out if our federal friend has his usual little surprise in store for you."

Lucas sat down in an armchair and looked at Kyle. "Raven is Josh's wife," he told her. "She's also Kelsey's ex-partner. Sarah is Rafferty's wife, and she currently works for Hagen's agency doing research. Unless—" He returned a questioning gaze to the lawyer.

"Her leave starts this week," Rafferty told him. "The baby's due next month."

Kyle looked at the men, puzzled. "Is this a group effort or what?"

"They're like that," Kelsey told her in a confiding tone. "Actually they were recruited when Josh met Raven in the middle of a sticky operation. Things just kind of snowballed from there. The bottom line is, Hagen found himself an almost unlimited source of unpaid manpower. He's been drafting these guys one at a time, but they all get into the act sooner or later." Kelsey blinked, then looked at Lucas. "I meant to ask, is Zach still on his honeymoon?"

"Supposed to be." Lucas lifted an eyebrow at Rafferty.

"Well . . ."

"Him too," Kelsey said, unsurprised.

"Dammit, Rafferty—"

"Hey, it's not my fault," Rafferty said dryly. "And Josh didn't tell him. He and Teddy got back to New York yesterday, and when you weren't around,

Zach knew you'd been drafted. Hell, he expected it."

Lucas shook his head but said, "Well, this time it can hardly be a group effort. Kyle can get me into Rome's house, but the rest of you—" Then he looked at her. "You know, you never said you would."

Ignoring the deeper question in his eyes, she said lightly, "I'm getting intrigued. So, why not?"

Plaintively Kelsey said, "And I'll have to skulk around as usual."

"On the estate?" Lucas asked him, looking away from Kyle with an obvious effort. "What about Rome's security?"

Mildly offended, Kelsey said, "You forget. Unlike you amateurs, I am a professional. Highly skilled and trained. With years of experience. I can pick any lock, disarm any bomb, finesse my way through any security system. My talents are vast, my stealth unsurpassed—"

"Thinks he's the Shadow," Rafferty murmured.

Finding himself the focus of fascinated eyes, Kelsey grinned suddenly and descended to normality. "And if all else fails," he said cheerfully, "I'll just shinny over the fence."

Lucas stared at him for a moment, then said suspiciously, "Just why'd you want a ride out here, anyway?"

Kelsey linked his fingers together over his flat stomach and leaned back, looking innocent again. "Well, Hagen just recently found a new bit of information he thought you should have. So that you'd be fully aware of all relevant facts in the case," he said blandly.

Lucas looked at Rafferty. "Did Raven and Sarah find out anything surprising?"

"Just one thing," the lawyer muttered, watching Kelsey.

Kelsey appeared hurt. "Stop staring at me like I'm on the witness stand," he told Rafferty severely. "I don't know what Raven and Sarah found out, but Hagen *has* promised to come clean this time."

"He usually doesn't," Lucas told Kyle.

"*Never* does," Rafferty amended.

"Well, this time he will," Kelsey stated. He looked at Lucas. "What he found out is that you may have to deal with a rather unpredictable character at Rome's estate. She appeared on the scene before the artwork was stolen, and she seems to have Rome completely under her thumb. But we have no idea what—if anything—she has to do with the theft."

"Who is she?" Lucas asked.

For the first time Kelsey seemed honestly uncomfortable. "Well, she apparently claims to be a reincarnated Aztec princess."

Lucas blinked. "Uh-huh."

"I swear."

Lucas looked at Rafferty, and the lawyer nodded. "It's true enough. Calls herself Princess Zamara. A somewhat flamboyant personality, to say the least."

"I thought Rome was supposed to be a hard-headed businessman," Lucas said in surprise. "You mean, he's buying her act?"

"How d'you know it's an act?" Kelsey asked.

Lucas stared at him.

Kelsey grinned. "All the way to the bank," he said. "He's spent a fortune on the woman in just a few weeks. She seems to have convinced him that his destiny is tied to the fortunes of the Aztecs. Or something like that."

Lucas turned his gaze to Kyle. "Does that sound like Rome?"

"No, not really. But I haven't seen him in six months." Kyle thought for a moment, then added slowly, "He always seemed to have a strong belief in fate, though. And after his first wife died about five years ago, rumor had it that he was consulting mediums pretty often. Still, I wouldn't have said he'd believe in reincarnated Aztec princesses."

Running a hand through his thick, silvery hair, Lucas muttered, "How's all this going to affect my job?"

"Beats me," Kelsey replied.

Rafferty stirred. "Zach had information for you. When we found out about this Zamara, he remembered that one piece of artwork stolen was a solid gold Aztec death mask. And Sarah did a little research. It seems this mask is supposed to confer enormous power on whoever owns it. It has quite a history too. Several owners—including two who stole it—amassed a great deal of wealth after it came into their possession. But the last owner lost everything he had, and the mask ended up in a museum. He was rumored to have said that the thing was cursed rather than blessed. It gathered dust in the museum until a couple of months ago when it was stolen, along with a truckload of other priceless gems and artwork."

For long minutes the only sound in the small cabin was the crackle of the fire. Then Lucas sighed and shook his head. "I don't believe in coincidence," he said. "Has anyone suggested Rome may have wanted that truckload of art just because the mask was one of the pieces?"

"It seems incredible," Kyle said. "You told me he'd paid for the artwork with a shipment of illegal arms. That sounds like an awfully complicated way to get his hands on the mask."

Rafferty said dryly, "Well, here's the kicker. Zach found out where Ryan was being held and went to see him this morning. Ryan," he added to Kyle, "was the ringleader of the art thieves. He and Zach have an odd sort of enmity. If it weren't for Zach and his new wife, Teddy, Ryan would probably still be running around loose, but he talked to Zach this morning."

Musingly Kelsey said, "We really should use Zach to interrogate prisoners more often. He scares me when he smiles."

Lucas gave him an impatient look, then asked Rafferty, "What did Ryan say?"

"He said—off the record—that he'd been commissioned to take everything in a certain room of the museum. Just for the hell of it, he took more, then upped his price. Originally he was supposed to be paid in cold, hard cash. He decided he wanted guns instead and demanded them."

"And got them?" Kyle asked, intrigued.

"Actually *we've* got them," Kelsey answered absently. "Thanks, I regret to say, to these clowns."

"I should have left you in jail," Rafferty told him.

"I wasn't in jail. I was being held incommunicado as a political prisoner."

"In a room with bars on the windows. That wasn't jail?"

"Just a highly security-conscious hotel."

Rafferty said something impolite.

"Can we get back to the point, please?" Lucas asked with awful patience.

"Gladly." Kelsey frowned at him. "What was it?"

Kyle choked back a laugh. Since Lucas seemed too irritated to respond, she murmured, "Um, I think it was that Martin apparently wanted just the mask."

"Well, he kept it all," Kelsey told them, serious again. "He hasn't moved anything larger than his car keys out of that house in weeks."

"Sure?" Rafferty asked.

Kelsey winced, as if the mild question had jabbed a sore spot. "Yes, dammit, I'm sure! Three agents have had the place under surveillance around the clock since the shipment got there."

"Don't you two get started again," Lucas warned the men.

Instantly transferring his attention to the blond man, Kelsey said, "You know, I've never seen you like this, Luc. Who licked the red off your candy?"

Kyle choked on a laugh.

Kelsey looked at her. "Have you been irritating our Lucas?" he asked sternly. "He's usually such a cheerful soul."

"Dammit, Kelsey!" Lucas snapped.

Undeterred, Kelsey said to Rafferty, "You've known him longer than I have. Is it the mountain air, d'you think?"

With a wary eye on his fuming friend, Rafferty said, "You'd carry a torch into a room full of gunpowder, Kelsey. Kyle, the only real talent Kelsey can claim is the ability to make coffee. I think we could all use some, if you wouldn't mind?"

"Of course." She rose and led the way into the kitchen, curious but a bit wary of the sudden undercurrents in the room.

When they were out of earshot, Lucas murmured, "Thanks."

"Don't mention it." Rafferty's voice was equally low. "He's right, though. You seem a little frayed around the edges."

Lucas didn't say anything for a moment, then sighed a bit roughly. "Ever have something from your past come back to haunt you?"

"We all have, I think." He studied his friend's suddenly haggard face, then said softly, "So Kyle's the one. I always thought there was someone you couldn't forget."

Lucas grimaced. "My great poker face."

"No, not your face," Rafferty told him. "Something in your eyes, maybe. This isn't going to be easy for you, is it?"

Gazing off toward the kitchen, Lucas murmured, "No more than I deserve."

"Can I help?"

"No." He shook his head. "But thanks."

In the kitchen, Kyle found that she was entirely comfortable with Kelsey, as if she'd known him forever. And that, she decided shrewdly, was probably a part of the man's effectiveness as an agent. He had the instinctive knack of putting people at ease, which made his behavior toward Lucas all the more surprising.

"Do you always needle Luc like that?" she asked, too curious to avoid the subject.

Kelsey was measuring coffee into the percolator and didn't answer until he'd finished. Then he leaned back against the counter and smiled at her. "Who, me? I was just making an observation."

She realized quite suddenly that despite his cheerful demeanor and his mischievous personality, this man was dangerous. She wasn't afraid of him but began to feel a bit wary because a part of his danger, she decided, lay in perceptiveness. She had the uneasy feeling that he saw people much more clearly than they would find at all comfortable—including herself.

"I'm harmless," Kelsey murmured.

Kyle started, then managed to hide her surprise. "That isn't the word I would have chosen," she said slowly.

He made a slight grimace, a bit wry but otherwise cryptic. "Maybe not. Doesn't fit you, either. You've got poor Lucas tied up in knots."

She stiffened. "That isn't your business."

Coolly he said, "I'm a government agent, Miss Griffon, and I take my job very seriously. I do my homework."

"Meaning?"

"Meaning that I know very well you and Luc have a history. Now, that *is* none of my business, except where this assignment is concerned. There's just one thing I wanted you to be aware of. He probably made it sound simple, but for Luc to go into Rome's house is one hell of a risky proposition. If Rome finds out who he is and what he's doing there, things are liable to get just a little ugly."

Quite suddenly Kyle felt cold. "What do you mean?"

"He could get killed."

"Martin's civilized," she objected instantly. "He wouldn't kill a man just like—"

"He has before."

She stared at him.

Kelsey nodded. "Oh, yes. We can't prove it in

court, you understand—no evidence. And he didn't
dirty his own hands with murder; he had it done,
which, to my mind, is the same as pulling the
trigger himself."

"Why did you tell me?" she asked after a moment.

"Because I knew Luc wouldn't."

"Does he know?"

"Of course he does." Kelsey smiled just a little,
but his eyes were steady. "He's very protective of
those he cares about—and uncommonly gallant
about ladies. He'll spare you the harsh realities
whenever possible."

He didn't before, she thought. Or had he? She
just didn't know anymore. Tightly she said, "I
don't need protection or chivalry."

"No, I didn't think you did." His voice was quite
cool and calm. "Unlike Luc, I've had the great
good fortune to work with a number of women in
dangerous situations over the years, and I've
learned that toughness comes in all shapes and
sizes. You see, I happen to believe you'll be a
greater help to him if you know just what he's
involved in."

"So now I know."

"Now you know. You don't entirely believe me
about Rome, of course, but you'll be more alert
than you would otherwise have been, and that
always counts for something."

She looked at him, a little puzzled. "And you
don't think—because of what I may believe now—
that I'll alert Martin that something's wrong by
behaving differently toward him?"

"Hell, no." Very dryly he explained, "It didn't
take me five minutes to realize you don't give
away anything."

Kyle couldn't protest that, as much as she wanted to. And though she didn't ask Kelsey, she had to wonder if she appeared as frozen as she felt. It wasn't a nice thought. It wasn't a nice feeling.

"I like your friends," she told Lucas late that afternoon when the other two had gone. She sat watching him as he knelt at the hearth building up the fire.

"Do you?" He remained where he was, brushing his hands together and gazing at the flames.

"They seem as though they're very unusual men."

Lucas rose but continued to gaze into the fire. He seemed far away.

"So do you," she added.

He turned his head to look at her and his mouth twisted. "We both know what you think of me."

"No, we don't, not really. Why didn't you tell me that Martin was dangerous, Luc?"

He didn't say anything for a moment, just continued to look at her. "Kelsey," he muttered finally.

"You wouldn't have told me. He knew that. He thought I should be prepared, and he was right."

"There was no need for you to know." Lucas returned his gaze to the fire, frowning.

Abruptly she asked, "Why did you have my father send me to Europe, Luc?"

"What makes you think I did? I don't know your father."

"And Josh Long doesn't know me. He's something of a humanitarian, I hear, but ten years ago he was also a playboy. So why did he concern himself then with a seventeen-year-old girl he'd never met? Unless someone asked him to."

After a moment Lucas said, "Josh is a good friend. He didn't know me very well at that time, but he didn't ask questions."

She heard the tacit admission and sighed. "Did you want an ocean between us, Luc, was that it?"

He closed his eyes briefly. "I wanted you off that campus, away from the drugs."

Kyle thought about that for a moment. He had left her to preserve an illusion between them, and yet he had done his best to protect her. He had destroyed evidence that would have taken her to court, if not to jail, had had her sent far away to a school where drugs were more rare than dinosaurs. It seemed a contradiction in character, and yet she felt it wasn't.

"I don't understand you," she said.

"Do you want to?"

"I already—"

"I know what you said."

She met his steady gaze, her own unwavering. "I meant it. I do want to understand you. I have to, Luc, or the past will never be—well, just the past."

He nodded, but she couldn't tell from his expression what he was thinking or feeling. He smiled suddenly, that faintly crooked, charming smile she remembered so well. "Then we go on from there, don't we?"

"I guess we do."

It was two days before she began to feel more natural around Lucas. She knew he was aware of her guardedness, just as she was aware that he watched her often. But gradually she began to feel less tense. It would have been too much to say that she forgot her wounds, but the past seemed to be retreating in importance, day by day.

The situation was helped in part by her preoccupation with discovering just who Lucas Kendrick really was. Instinct told her he was a good man, whatever had motivated him in the past, but she found it difficult to trust her instincts where he was concerned. So she watched him, asked questions, and listened.

Her one legacy from her father, given to her in the childhood days when she had tried to win his affection, was an ability to understand and play chess, and she recalled that her father had often said a man's chess game spoke much about the kind of man he really was. So she played chess with Lucas, unsurprised to find that he did play, and played well.

He had a strong instinctive grasp of tactics, she discovered, and the ability to make seemingly reckless intuitive leaps virtually guaranteed to take his opponent off guard. He was a gracious winner, a cheerful loser.

In the following days she found out other things about him. He didn't mind silence. He enjoyed walking in the light covering of snow, chopping wood, listening to music. He could cook, and did, and he did more than his share to help keep the cabin neat. He could stand so still sometimes that a wild bird would alight and eat bread crumbs from his hand with perfect trust.

He had nightmares.

Kyle awoke twice that first week, hearing mutters and muffled groans from downstairs, hearing him toss and turn on the couch. The sounds haunted her, disturbed her deeply. But she didn't go to him then and said nothing about what she had heard.

The third time, halfway through their second week together, she did go to him.

The first rasping groan woke her, and she was out of her bed and moving lightly down the stairs before she had time to think or question her action. She hesitated for just a moment at the bottom of the stairs, wondering why she had to do this.

The room was dim, lighted only by the dying flames in the hearth, and outside the wind whined with a lonely, fretful sound. Kyle bit her lip, undecided, and would have returned to her bed but for the soft, unsteady groan that reached her ears then. She crossed the room on quick, bare feet, and knelt on the rug beside the couch.

A half-burned log broke apart in the hearth just then with a shower of sparks, and the flames jumped higher. She could see Lucas more clearly. The covers had fallen to his waist, leaving his muscled chest bare, and his body was so tense, it trembled slightly. A fine sheen of sweat beaded his face. One forearm was thrown across his eyes, fist clenched; his other arm lay at his side, and his fingers held the covers in a white-knuckled grip. His throat worked as if sounds or words or some darkness inside him struggled to escape, but only the low groans were released from his sleeping prison.

Kyle looked at the strong hand gripping the blankets, then hesitantly covered it with one of her own. It felt like iron, she thought, burning iron, and feeling that made her hurt oddly. She bent closer, uncertain but driven, unwilling to allow him to go through whatever this was all alone.

"Luc? Luc, wake up," she said softly.

"Behind the building," he muttered suddenly, urgently. "He ran behind— Oh, dear Lord! The dumpster. He just threw her in there. *Why can't I stop this*? Why can't I—"

"Luc, wake up!"

He jerked suddenly, and his hand turned beneath hers, long fingers closing tightly around hers. He was still for a moment, and then the arm over his eyes lowered. He looked at her, disoriented. "You aren't a part of that," he said thickly.

"Luc, it's just a dream," she whispered.

His eyes cleared slowly but continued to move over her face almost searchingly. "No. No, it happened. It happened and I couldn't change it."

"Then tell me about it."

He tore his gaze from her face, staring at the beamed ceiling. After a moment he said, "It was the first time. I suppose after that—God help me—I got used to it. There was a woman—a kid, really— busted for possession. The D.A. promised to go easy on her if she'd give us her supplier. She agreed. But he found the wire, and we were too far back to help her. We . . . found her in a garbage dumpster. He had stabbed her."

Kyle's surface recklessness had taken her into some wild places these last years, but what he was telling her about was a part of life she had no experience of, except in fiction and coolly reported news stories. She felt a little helpless, overwhelmed by the pain she heard. "Luc, it was your job."

"It was a war of attrition," he said bitterly. "But

the problem was, the other side kept on growing. Fourteen-year-old pushers, twelve-year-old prostitutes, pimps who'd kill one of their girls without a second thought because there were always more so easily found."

Kyle was silent.

"There was no way to make a difference," he went on quietly. He pulled her hand over to rest on his flat stomach, holding it with both his own and looking at it. "Maybe I could have kept on trying, I don't know. But too often I'd be told to stop nosing around a certain party. Somebody rich enough, or powerful enough, to have *friends* in the department. Too many people playing too many games. I couldn't take that."

"No one could blame you," she ventured hesitantly.

He was toying with her fingers, stroking her skin as if the texture drew him irresistibly. "Feet of clay," he murmured. "I couldn't be the white knight, so I just quit."

"Don't do this to yourself."

His mouth twisted a little. "It never bothered me so much before. Then I saw you again and had to face up to why I left you. And now I'm dreaming of things I saw all those years ago and wondering how I can live with myself."

Kyle searched for something to say to him and found it. "Luc, you told me about the work you do for Long Enterprises. You're helping people now where you *can* make a difference. You help keep all those companies running by investigating problems. You and your friends helped destroy a white slavery ring, brought information against terrorists out of a hostile country, and stopped that gun shipment before it could be used to hurt people. And now you're about to go into a house and find stolen artwork. You *are* helping. There are over half a million police officers in this country; you're doing things they can't do."

After a moment he turned his head to look at her and smiled a little, a smile that made him vulnerable. "You gave me a wonderful illusion ten years ago when I really needed one," he said huskily. "But I don't think I could stand it if you gave me another one now, Kyle."

"I don't do that anymore," she said, her own voice unsteady. "All I can give you now is a picture of a real live man. One I've talked to and watched these past days. An extremely bright, intricate man, with more facets than a diamond." She drew a deep breath and met his shimmering gaze squarely. "I don't know how I feel about what's behind us. But there is something I know now about you, Luc."

One of his hands moved to brush a strand of dark hair away from her face, his fingers lingering on her cheek. "What's that?"

"There isn't a selfish or dishonest bone in your body," she said with certain knowledge. "When you realized yourself why you'd left me, you didn't have to tell me. But you did. And I see now that you couldn't be honest with me then, first because you were undercover and later because of the way I was. The way we were. You were in a terrible position. And I believe I understand why you left."

"You do?" he asked gently.

Her laugh was shaky, almost inaudible. "I'm not painting you noble again, I promise. And I still don't know how I feel about you now. But we were both escaping into illusion, I think. We'd both felt things we didn't want to feel anymore. You in your job and me . . ."

"Your family?"

"Poor little rich girl," she said wryly, mocking herself.

"Don't do that." His hand slid beneath her hair to lie warmly against her neck. "Don't think it's your fault in any way, that you should have been happy just because you had all the so-called advantages. Material things are never enough."

He pulled her toward him and kissed her, a gentle kiss with no passionate demand. Then he held her there, against him, watching the firelight shimmer off her silk pajamas and awaken the red tint in her dark hair.

Kyle could feel tremors deep inside her, circling outward slowly, like ripples in a pool. She didn't know what had caused them and didn't care. The wind whined outside, moaning around the eaves, stirring the porch swing so that the chains creaked. She heard every sound more clearly than ever before.

And she could see awareness flickering in his eyes. It was as if something were moving with hushed force inside both of them, slowly and inexorably. Fascinated, she watched his face change subtly, become leaner, tauter. She felt that gentle hand on her neck tighten a little, and underneath her own hand his stomach tensed.

Very softly he said, "Kyle, go back upstairs."

"Why?" she asked huskily.

He seemed to be having trouble breathing, but his voice was steady. "Because I love you."

Kyle slowly rose to her feet, compelled by something in his eyes or his voice, or both. She turned away and went silently back up the stairs, sliding into her bed and drawing the covers up. She lay there for a long time with her eyes fixed on the dark ceiling, listening to the wind outside. And thinking.

What would they have lost if they had become lovers again tonight? Kyle wasn't sure, but she knew Lucas thought he was, and that was why he had sent her back to bed alone. What was it? A new and fragile thread of trust between them? A delicate bond forged in the quiet, soul-baring moments after a nightmare?

Kyle turned over on her side and closed her eyes, hardly aware that she was smiling.

Four

"I don't trust you," Kelsey told his boss roundly. "You're just acting too damned straightforward."

Hagen, sitting behind a desk that held nothing but a thin sheaf of papers and a telephone with several lines, looked up to smile angelically. "You have a suspicious mind, my boy."

Kelsey saluted him mockingly. "Learned at the master's knee." He leaned back in the single visitor's chair in the room and stared broodingly at Hagen. "As far as I can tell, you've been completely straight with Lucas. So what gives?"

"Nothing at all, I assure you." Hagen feigned humility—something he didn't do too well. "Kendrick deserves all the facts; I merely supplied them."

"Uh-huh." Kelsey pointed at the sheaf of papers on the desk. "Just out of curiosity, whose idea was it that Josh innocently call Rome to inquire about the possibility of buying that Rubens and subsequently try to get himself invited to the party?"

"His. And sound strategy, I must admit. His interest in the painting is quite real; he's known to acquire anything by Rubens that becomes available. And, of course, it was a good thing he got invited to the party. Should Rome be suspicious, he will keep a sharp eye on Long."

"Leaving Luc free to search for the stolen art?" Kelsey kept his gaze fixed thoughtfully on the revised guest list for Martin Rome's party.

"That is the plan," Hagen told him.

"And you don't think Rome will panic and move the stuff because he knows Josh is coming?"

"Not enough time. And if he does attempt to move the artwork, we'll have him dead to rights."

Kelsey lifted his eyes to Hagen's cherubic face. "A nice, simple plan. I must be asleep and dreaming."

"Why don't you go and call Kendrick," Hagen suggested. "He should be told that Long and Raven will attend the party. Also, you must arrange your nightly rendezvous with the lady and him. All those little details to work out, my boy."

Rising slowly, Kelsey frowned at his boss. "You missed the human element again," he reminded him with a certain satisfaction. "Whatever happened between Luc and Kyle years ago, I'd say they're busy mending fences now."

Coolly Hagen said, "An entirely anticipated development."

Kelsey blinked. "You mean this time you deliberately set the scene for a romance?"

"Certainly."

After a moment Kelsey asked, "You decided to stop matchmaking by accident and do it on purpose?"

Maddeningly impervious to his agent's surprise, Hagen merely nodded.

"Why?"

"To find out if I could."

Kelsey blinked again. "Oh." He turned and went to the door, then swung around to frown at his boss. "Are you feeling all right?" he asked.

"I'm fine. Go call Kendrick."

When his baffled agent had finally vanished, Hagen leaned back in his chair and laughed softly. Every general knew how effective the element of surprise could be, after all. Let them wonder and look over their shoulders for his customary surprise. They would look in vain, he thought happily. And that would be the surprise. It would keep them all on their toes.

Hagen enjoyed keeping his agents on their toes.

Kyle unpacked in the luxurious room she had been given in Martin Rome's palatial house just outside Philadelphia, having politely refused the assistance of a maid; there were some things she preferred to do for herself. She moved around the room briskly, speculating on various things, and wasn't surprised when Lucas spoke from the connecting door to his room.

"Is this arrangement supposed to be discreet?"

She smiled a little as she stood before the dressing table, watching him in the mirror as she removed the pins from her hair. "More discreet, I suppose, than giving us a single room or letting us sneak into each other's through the hall in the dead of night. Martin obviously assumes we wouldn't have shown up together if we didn't want to be together."

Lucas leaned against the doorjamb, watching

her dark hair tumble down around her shoulders. Absently he said, "Well, Rome didn't seem too upset when you arrived with me. Think this mysterious Zamara has captured his heart as well as his mind?"

"We'll have to wait and see. She might well be 'indisposed' at the moment and unable to greet guests, but I'm betting she's going to make a suitably dramatic entrance tonight." Kyle turned to face him, leaning back against the dresser. "When are Mr. Long and his wife arriving?"

"A little later, I think. Kelsey wasn't sure. Just remember you are supposed to know Josh—and introduce us."

"Do I know his wife?" she asked dryly.

Lucas smiled at her. "Yes, you know Raven. Rome shouldn't think that odd at all. Josh and Raven will be delighted to see you again, and I'll be merely your escort."

"And lover," she murmured. Before he could respond, she went on calmly. "Your background is that you're from a West Coast family in the wine business, we met on a skiing holiday at Aspen, and you swept me off my feet."

"Precisely."

"So. When do we start searching?"

"Kyle, we've been through this be—"

"And I say my way makes more sense. Luc, if you're caught skulking through the house on your own, it'll look suspicious. As if you were casing the joint, at the very least. If I'm with you, we can always give the appearance we were overwhelmed by passion and had to find a dark corner to neck in."

"Don't tempt me."

Kyle slowly crossed the room to stand before him. "Maybe I want to. What happens on Monday, Luc?"

He looked down at her, thinking of the past days when both had been so careful not to disturb the fragile harmony between them. And he felt the throbbing ache that was always with him now, heating his blood and clouding his mind. It was dangerous, what he was feeling. Dangerous because he would need to be alert and aware, and he could hardly think of anything except Kyle.

But he had made up his mind that he would give Kyle all the time she needed. If he had to take cold showers every hour, he was still determined that the choice would be hers.

Resisting the nearly overpowering urge to yank her into his arms, he said, "That depends on what you want to happen."

"You'll have to go back to New York, won't you?"

"I have weeks of vacation time coming to me. Things are pretty calm at the office now, so I can take the time off if I want. Why don't we wait until Monday?"

"Business before pleasure?" she asked lightly.

"Not necessarily." He wondered what she was feeling. As always, it was impossible to tell from her lovely face or turquoise eyes. With a sudden intuition he knew that when he *could* find some hint of her thoughts just by looking at her, the past would be buried for good. The knowledge was little consolation. She was as enigmatic as a cat, and those creatures had kept their secrets for thousands of years.

She was looking at him now, her expression still unreadable. "Well," she said, "I'm unpacked. How about you?"

"Yes."

"Then why don't we explore a bit? Martin did offer us the run of the house."

Lucas thought about that and had to admit it sounded like a good idea. There would be about fifty guests during the weekend, most of them scheduled to come during the next few hours. The activity of arriving guests and servants provided them with the perfect time to explore.

"Fine." They went out into the hall from her room—and found themselves face-to-face with their host.

Martin Rome was slender and just over six feet tall. He had black hair with wings of silver at the temples, rather penetrating dark eyes, and a handsome, distinguished-looking face that appeared a decade younger than his forty-five years. He also had a pleasant, deep voice and charming manners. And those manners were evident when he said nothing at all about their exit from Kyle's bedroom or about the inherent possessiveness of Luc's hand resting at the small of Kyle's back.

"Settled in?" he asked graciously.

Kyle smiled at him, a smile that was a little more than social manners and a little less than intimacy. "Yes, thanks, Martin. I wanted to show Luc some of your wonderful art collection, if that's all right."

"Certainly. Pay close attention in the trophy room, Kyle. I've recently acquired some splendid examples of primitive fertility statuettes." He met Lucas's gaze briefly, his own bland, then moved on down the hall.

Kyle tucked her hand in his arm and turned him in the opposite direction, saying, "This way, darling," in a voice that was subtly different from the voice she had used with Rome.

Lucas obeyed the guiding touch, but something deep inside him was jangling an alarm. "Trophy room?" he said distractedly. "For fertility statues?"

"Gives you an idea how his mind works," Kyle murmured. "He's been collecting those things for years, and they've always been displayed in the trophy room. Interesting, isn't it?"

"You've been here before," Lucas realized, and in that moment he knew why his instincts had growled warningly.

She looked up at him curiously as they made their way down a wide, curving staircase to the ground floor of the mansion. "Many times," she confirmed. "I suppose I assumed you knew that. Actually I came here first as a child. My parents visited Martin several times a year."

Evenly Lucas asked, "When did he plan to marry you? Then?"

Kyle was frowning a bit but continued to lead him across the foyer and down a short hall. She didn't respond until they entered a room that was filled with an astonishing collection of animal skins, weapons, figurines, headdresses—and just about anything else that a primitive society could have considered a trophy. And even a few things that more enlightened societies had prized, such as animal-skin rugs.

She released Luc's arm and wandered around the room, gazing with little interest at the displays.

"Kyle?"

Avoiding any touch of the polar-bear skin on the polished hardwood floor, she moved past it and then paused, staring at a collection of knives in a glass case. "He was married then," she said.

Lucas allowed his gaze to roam around the room, but he paid little attention to the collections. Still, he felt oddly savage, an unfamiliar sensation, and wondered distantly if the violence implicit in the room was having an effect on him. "That's not an answer," he told her finally.

She turned to look at him, surprised by the harshness in his voice. "Luc, what's wrong?"

"He wants you," Lucas said baldly. "I don't know what kind of hold this Zamara has on him, but he wants *you*."

Kyle glanced toward the door, then moved to stand before him as the distant sounds of a new set of arrivals were heard. "I told you about water dropping on stone, remember?"

Lucas kept his hands in the pockets of his slacks, but he was far more tense than he looked. "You told me. I suppose I'd forgotten that when we learned about Zamara. But I shouldn't have done so. Rome would never marry a woman like her, would he, Kyle? No matter who she *says* she is, she just doesn't have the blue-blood lines he feels are necessary for his wife."

She was looking up at him, and shook her head briefly. "No. Martin would never disgrace his family name by marrying out of his class. That's garbage, of course, but it still holds true for many families. His is one of them."

"How about yours?"

Lightly but with an undertone of bitterness she said, "I've already disgraced mine through the years." Then she shrugged. "Luc, what is all this?"

Her back was to the door, Lucas facing her, and when he caught a glimpse of movement, he acted without thinking at all. And maybe it was with the intention of demonstrating to Martin Rome that Kyle was no longer unattached that he acted, but it took no more than a few seconds to make reasoning unimportant.

The soft sweater she was wearing caressed his hands as he touched it, and the warm, firm flesh beneath was a balm to his hungry senses. He pulled her against him and bent his head to meet her startled lips with his own. Kyle was stiff in his arms for only an instant, and then she melted against him.

He felt her mouth opening to him, her hands slipping up around his neck. He felt the firm mounds of her breasts against his chest where two sweaters were frail barriers between heated bodies. And he felt the slow building of a potent, raw, and powerful force inside him.

The dark, spicy scent of her perfume rose from her skin to fill his mind with its seductive promise, and he drew her more tightly against him, one hand sliding down her back to press her hips to the aching fullness of his loins.

He heard a soft sound then and didn't know if he had made it or if she had. A low, hungry sound that was almost pain. Wanting her had become a driving compulsion, all else forgotten. With so much still uncertain between them he needed the certainty of knowing she could feel desire for him. He wanted to see her face lose its enigmatic serenity in the primitive heat of passion, wanted to feel her go wild beneath him, her body holding him deep inside her.

If he had felt caution, he would have thrown it to the winds; if there had been any awareness of his surroundings, he would have mused that the bearskin rug would make a fine bed; if he had considered the danger of his mission in this house, it would have been no more than a fleeting, disinterested thought. But Lucas felt nothing except the woman in his arms and his own violent need, was aware of nothing else, thought of nothing else.

But in the distance he heard a voice.

"Ah, we seem to be intruding on two of my other guests. Perhaps I could show you the trophy room later?"

Another voice. "We know Kyle; perhaps she'll forgive us for interrupting. I believe I hear more of your guests arriving, Martin."

"If you'll excuse me—?"

"Certainly."

Footsteps going away. Footsteps coming into the room.

Lucas didn't know where he'd been, but he was an awfully long time returning to the primitive vibrations of the room and a niggling awareness of a hardwood floor beneath his feet. His eyelids felt impossibly heavy, and his heart seemed to have swelled tremendously because he could feel the runaway pounding throughout his entire body. And the slenderness of Kyle's warm body was a lifeline, something he'd have to hold on to or he'd drown . . . or burn up . . . or fly away somewhere and crash because he didn't have wings.

"Hello?"

He opened his eyes slowly, staring down into her dazed face. And he felt a flicker of intense pleasure because she was no longer serene and enigmatic. Her eyes shimmered darkly with desire, and her face was flushed, wondering. One of her hands moved from around his neck and touched his face lightly, carefully.

"They aren't listening."

"Listening? They aren't on the same planet!"

"You used to look at me like that."

"Used to?"

"Hey, how about that? You still do."

"This room is perfect for an orgy."

"Later, darling. Josh!"

"What?"

"How do you know what an orgy room should look like?"

"I must have seen a picture in a book."

"I don't believe you. I'll bet you had a harem of blondes and they threw orgies every Thursday."

"Certainly not."

"No?"

"On Saturday night, peasant."

"I want a divorce."

Silence.

"Well, maybe I'll stay married to you."

"I thought you might."

"Vain. The man is so vain. Kyle? Hello, Kyle?"

Vaguely aware of noises, Kyle removed her gaze from Lucas's pale face and turned her head slowly. It took her a moment to accept fully the presence of two people in the room with them, and she stared at them bemusedly.

The man was tall and broad-shouldered, with dark hair and slightly cool but amused blue eyes. He was also quite strikingly handsome and looked more formal than most men would in dark slacks, a white shirt open at the throat, and a black leather jacket zipped halfway up.

The woman standing in the circle of his right

arm was also tall and dark; she had long blue-black hair worn casually loose, and her face was lovely despite its not being beautiful. She had merry violet eyes and a warm smile, and the casual sweater and skirt she wore did terrific things for her splendid figure.

"Hi, Kyle," the woman said gently. "Remember us?"

Kyle blinked and thought about it. There were things expected of her. She was supposed to . . . what was she supposed to do? Oh, yes.

"Hello," she said dreamily. "I want you to meet Lucas Kendrick. This is Raven and Josh Long, Luc." She wondered if she had gotten that right. Odd how automatic knowledge seemed to have deserted her. Not that she cared. She looked back up at Lucas, then gently turned his head toward the others. "Say hello, Luc."

He blinked and stared at them. "Hello."

"At least he didn't say hello, Luc," Josh murmured, then looked down at his wife with a frown. "Never say I was that bad."

"No?" She smiled at him. "There wasn't a mirror handy when you were stretched out on the floor at my feet."

"True."

"Or when—"

"Never mind. I'll concede the point."

Lucas found himself the focus of the other man's gaze and wondered why he wasn't the least bit self-conscious. It seemed entirely natural to be standing there with his arms around Kyle. But he realized gradually that something was expected of him, so he asked, "Where's Rome?"

"Greeting guests," Josh told him. "I think we're safe for the moment."

"Maybe you are," Lucas murmured.

"This is very hard going," Josh told his wife despairingly.

"I know, but they'll be completely with us soon. Do you think he'd hit me if I took her away from him?"

Josh looked thoughtful. "He'd hit me if I did."

"We'll go for a walk in the garden," Raven decided. She took Kyle gently by the arm and drew her away from Lucas. "Kyle, do you know the key to the maze? I've heard Rome has a wonderful maze in his garden."

Kyle looked at her. "Oh. Yes."

"Good enough," Raven murmured, laughter in her eyes. She looked at her husband as she led Kyle past him. "I think you'd better get Luc a drink. We'll be in the center of the maze, darling. You two come and find us a little later."

"I found my way through one maze to get you," Josh told her severely.

"Chin up, darling. This one's only made of bushes."

"Well, all right. But leave a trail of bread crumbs."

When the women had gone, Josh left briefly himself, returning with a strong drink for his friend. Lucas hadn't even noticed Josh's absence.

Kyle wasn't accustomed to confiding in anyone. She had friends all over the world, but none really knew her. Her mother's sense of decorum had been drummed into her: A lady never betrayed having strong emotions—if she had them, and even having them was bad form; a lady never raised her voice for any reason and certainly never cried in public. A lady kept her problems to herself always, no matter what. And, above all, a lady was never—not under any circumstances—to be seen embracing any man in front of anyone, servants, friends, or strangers. Heaven forbid that she should embrace a man *passionately*.

Her own and her brother's existences as proof to the contrary, Kyle had always been certain that her mother didn't believe it was proper to embrace a man in private, either. Even a husband.

Kyle was, of course, very different from her mother. Yet still she had heard her mother's strictures all too often, and for too many years, not to be conscious of breaking one of those rules.

So she should have felt definitely embarrassed at having met Raven Long and her husband for the first time while she was so dazed with desire that she'd hardly been coherent. She could hear her mother's voice, apalled, condemning, ringing in her mind.

And she didn't give a damn.

By the time they reached the center of the maze, with Raven merely strolling along beside her in silence, Kyle had recovered her wits. She didn't know what had happened between her and Lucas in the trophy room, but whatever it was, she wasn't embarrassed about it. Bewildered, elated, half frightened, doubtful, eager, wary, excited—but not embarrassed.

In the center of the maze, surrounded by eight-foot walls of green hedge, was a lovely white gazebo with curving, padded benches inside. Kyle had automatically led them here with no thought of the correct turns; she had memorized the maze in childhood and often had sat in the gazebo for hours, alone with her thoughts.

Raven looked around her with pleasure as they stepped up into the gazebo and sat on the bench. "This is wonderful. Did Rome have the maze designed?"

Kyle, studying the other woman, shook her head. "No. His grandfather, I believe."

"I didn't think he was playful enough for something like this. Do you know him well?"

"A long time—but not well."

The merry violet eyes glanced briefly at her, and Kyle felt just as she had with Kelsey. This woman, she thought, was highly perceptive. And strong. That much was clearly visible behind the laughing eyes. Perhaps even dangerous in the right situation—or the wrong one. Then Kyle remembered that Raven had been Kelsey's partner.

". . . toughness comes in all shapes and sizes," he had said about past female partners.

Kyle felt comfortable with Raven Long, but her voice was nonetheless gruff when she murmured, "I don't know what happened to me back there."

"Don't you?" Raven was gazing off into space, her eyes distant and thoughtful.

"No, I—" Kyle bit her lip. "Yes. Yes, I know. But it was never like that before, not even with Luc. I've never felt that way in my life."

Raven half turned on the bench and looked at the younger woman with an open but neutral expression, inviting confidence but not asking. "Kyle, I don't know what happened between you and Luc years ago—I only know that something *did* happen, something neither of you can forget."

Kyle shifted uneasily, and Raven spoke again in her warm, musical voice.

"Oh, Luc doesn't wear his heart on his sleeve,

and neither do you. He doesn't talk about himself, either. But I've been around him a good deal the last year or so, and I've seen. He goes out with women from time to time, but there's never more than a flicker of interest before those dates, then nothing at all afterward. Josh says he's been that way for ten years." Softly she added, "He carries a picture of you in his wallet, did you know? I saw it by accident one day. You were much younger then. And you were laughing."

She hadn't known, and Kyle felt hot tears dammed up behind her eyes. But she didn't cry. She hadn't cried for a long time. After a moment, in a voice devoid of emotion, she began telling Raven what had happened ten years ago. She spared neither Lucas nor herself in the telling, because she had to talk about it. Quite suddenly and with no ability to fight it, the need to talk rose up powerfully and pulled things out of her that no one except Lucas had ever known. It was a needed release, a thaw of emotions held frozen and at bay too long.

Raven was silent throughout, her expression compassionate and understanding. Then, when Kyle's voice had stilled, she began talking herself.

"I used to believe that love was something gentle and kind, something warm and comforting. But that was a very long time ago. The work I chose after I left school was . . . well, difficult. It was a life made up of lies and deceit, with no room for friends or family and no time for uncertainty. Josh says I walked in the shadows of dark streets and he's right. I had to be different people, terrible people, to do my job. I had to submerge everything I really was, everything I felt. And because of that, I was always afraid of losing who I was, afraid of having my true self slip away or change . . . for the worse. So I built careful walls around the innermost part of myself. A lot like the walls your family built around you. They expected you to be something you weren't, something you couldn't be, and I had to be something I wasn't. We were both hiding inside walls."

"Did you break out?" Kyle asked, remembering her own dam-burst of emotions.

"Yes." Then, softly, she said, "Thanks to Josh. That man taught me more about trust than most people learn in a lifetime. I didn't expect his trust, I had no right to. I didn't even believe in it. The evidence against me was damning, and any other man would have thought me worse than a . . . a whore. But Josh loved me in the face of all odds and despite evidence against me that he couldn't disprove even with all his money and power and connections."

"How lucky you are," Kyle murmured.

Quietly Raven said, "He wasn't an undercover cop with all the lies on his side. And I wasn't a seventeen-year-old as desperately fragile as a baby bird teetering on the edge of its nest."

Kyle was silent.

"Think about it," Raven urged. "As hard as it was for you to wake up alone and bewildered, you could soften the pain with all those idealistic, romantic dreams that young girls cling to. But Luc didn't have that option. He had walked dark streets and seen terrible things, and he didn't believe in dreams."

"He believed my illusion."

"Did he? No, Kyle. I know how he felt—because

I felt that way with Josh at first. I felt so dirty and hurt inside by what I'd seen, what I'd done, and Josh looked at me with a kind of love I didn't even believe in anymore. But I cherished the way he looked at me, because it was so far above what my life was. I was lucky. Josh was stronger than I was, and determined, and he was patient because he believed so completely in what we felt for each other.

"But Luc, what could he do, Kyle? Tell you about those dark streets and shadows, yank you from that nest you *had* to climb out of yourself? Tell you he wasn't what you thought he was? At that age it hurts so much worse to lose a dream than something real. He knew that. And he was going to hurt you, no matter what he did. He knew that too. It must have been hell for him on the last night with you. He loved something so fragile, he knew he'd destroy it if he stayed, change it irrevocably if he left."

Both women were silent for long minutes, Kyle gazing ahead of her with hot, inward-turned eyes and Raven watching her quietly. And then Raven spoke again.

"He did what he had to, you know. In an impossible situation he picked the option least damaging to you. Whatever his reasoning was then or now, he tried not to hurt you any more than he had to. He was probably afraid to get in touch with you later, afraid you'd never forgive the hurt or that you wouldn't be interested in the real man. Then the months turned into years and you had been apart too long."

"Then Hagen called," Kyle said slowly.

Raven nodded. "Giving him an excuse to see

you again—and even the best of men have to deal with their pride. He had a reason—a business-like, impersonal reason—and the rest depended on you."

Struggling to understand, Kyle said, "But when he left me, he believed I'd been buying and selling drugs."

"Is that what he told you?"

"He said that he wasn't sure, that perhaps he'd been more afraid then of me being disillusioned by him than of him being disappointed in me. I see now why he wasn't willing to confront me with it, to ask me. But he *could* have asked without really telling me about himself. Couldn't he?"

"Would it have changed anything if he had confronted you?"

"I don't know. Maybe. I think it wouldn't have changed anything between us, but my brother—"

"That idol would have fallen off his pedestal a little sooner," Raven said. "But you wouldn't have been able to help your brother, Kyle, not even if you'd known. People who use and push drugs just don't respond to loving concern. Believe that."

"People quit drugs."

"Yes. Would he have quit?"

After a moment Kyle sighed. "No. Not Dorian."

"Then nothing would have changed even if you'd known."

"It's so complicated."

Raven smiled. "Love always is. It's caring for someone more than you care for yourself. And Luc hurt himself more than he hurt you ten years ago. He left you alone and confused, yes, but you were capable of building your own illusion and keeping it safe, Kyle. He made himself walk away from that brief, beautiful illusion you gave him, and he wasn't capable of healing the wound with lovely dreams."

"Where does that leave us now?" Kyle looked at the woman who had also walked dark streets, wondering if it was possible to understand the grinding heartache of a life such as that without living it yourself.

"He came back to you," Raven reminded.

"He had to. He wasn't given a choice."

"There are always choices. Hagen's plan was the simplest but not the only one. Lucas went up to your cabin because he wanted to, Kyle. He wanted to see you again, whatever it cost him. Can you imagine what kind of courage that took? For all he knew, you could have despised him. He had no reason to believe you wouldn't. At best, he knew he'd have to face pain again. The pain of memories."

Kyle remembered a white, haggard face and a quiet, deep voice opening old wounds and exposing new ones in vulnerability. "I—I know. He says he loves me."

"Of course he loves you. He never would have walked away if he hadn't then. He wouldn't have come back if he didn't now."

It was so complicated, such a raging mass of conflicting emotions and memories and dreams, and Kyle didn't know if she could absorb it all. But as she sat there in the peaceful gazebo, feeling the crisp early-winter breeze, something inside her opened up and she felt a peculiar little flutter like the brush of soft wings. The churning confusion eased, leaving her feeling battered but calm.

"It isn't easy to trust," she said.

"No," Raven agreed. "Not easy at all. But some

things are worth the gamble, Kyle. He loves you. And I think . . . if you can put away those pretty dreams of knights on white chargers, you'll find something a seventeen-year-old girl could never even imagine. Chargers are outdated, you know—white or otherwise. And modern knights tend to be unsung heroes. They do quiet, dangerous things sometimes. They love and hurt and bleed. They even make mistakes."

"I know." And she did. For the first time she did.

Raven got to her feet and stood for a moment, looking down at Kyle. Softly she said, "Idols that fall off pedestals don't always break. Sometimes they get up and brush all that glittering dust away—and you find out they're just as tall without something to stand on."

Kyle looked at her and smiled. "Thank you."

Smiling in return, Raven said, "I have a good memory for mazes. I'll go meet Josh and Luc and tell him where you are."

"I *hate* mazes!" Josh said with considerable feeling, batting at a protruding arm of greenery. "How long have we been lost in this one?"

"Hours." Lucas was equally disgusted and quite definitely edgy. "What is Raven telling her?"

Josh paused to contemplate a dead end, muttered a curse as they retraced their steps, then looked at his friend. "How should I know?"

"Well, she's yours, after all."

"Be that as it may," Josh said, "I can hardly read her mind. Especially not with four acres of bushes between us. Just thank your luck she's not with Serena."

America's most popular, most compelling romance novels...

Here, at last...love stories that really involve you! Fresh, finely crafted novels with story lines so believable you'll feel you're actually living them! Characters you can relate to...exciting places to visit...unexpected plot twists...all in all, exciting romances that satisfy your mind and delight your heart.

EXAMINE 6 LOVESWEPT NOVELS FOR

15 Days FREE!

To introduce you to this fabulous service, you'll get six brand-new Loveswept releases not yet in the bookstores. These six exciting new titles are yours to examine for 15 days without obligation to buy. Keep them if you wish for just $12.50 plus postage and handling and any applicable sales tax.

Get one full-length Loveswept FREE every month!
Now you can be sure you'll never, ever miss a single
Loveswept title by enrolling in our special reader's home
delivery service. A service that will bring you all six new
Loveswept romances each month for the price of five—and
deliver them to you before they appear in the bookstores!

Examine 6 Loveswept Novels for
15 days FREE!
(SEE OTHER SIDE FOR DETAILS)

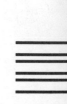

Mentally Lucas did. Fate had at least been kind to spare him the intervention of Josh's sister. Serena had a heart of gold, with an unnerving subtlety and the force of a Sherman tank.

They came to an intersection and stood staring at three possible avenues of progress.

"Which way did we come?"

"That way. No—that way. Hell, I don't know."

"We could sink our pride and start yelling," Josh suggested.

"I will if you will."

"This way," Josh decided firmly, heading down the middle path.

Minutes later, exiting again, Lucas said, "Buy this maze so we can burn it."

"It's not worth the match. Got any bread crumbs?"

"Not on me, no."

"Pity."

Five

Overhearing this conversation from three feet away on the other side on the hedge, Raven enjoyed it so much that she retraced her own steps back to the center and told Kyle about it. And Kyle, feeling more lighthearted than she had in years, went back with the other woman to eavesdrop shamelessly on the men. Both women enlarged their respective vocabularies of colorful curses, even Raven widening her eyes at some of her husband's phrases.

"And you think you know a man after living with him for a while," she murmured.

Soft as her voice was, it caught her husband's attention.

"It's Raven. She's over there."

"The whole world's over there," Lucas said irritably. And, a moment later, "There isn't any way to *get* over there. Kyle? Are you with Raven?"

"Of course I am, Luc," she called back.

"At the center?"

Raven laughed. "Sorry, guys, you aren't even halfway there. We got bored and came to find you."

"Well, find us!" her husband commanded.

Raven murmured something to Kyle, who nodded and vanished back into the greenery. Then Raven walked four steps right, turned left, and walked two more steps. She smiled. "Hello."

"You enjoyed that," Josh accused.

"Immensely. Luc, if you want Kyle, I can tell you how to find her. You *do* want her, don't you?"

Lucas stared into limpid violet eyes. "Yes, Raven," he said with strained patience. "I want Kyle. Where is she?"

"In the center." Raven gave him precise directions, then watched him turn a corner and disappear.

"If you weren't my dear and only love," Josh told her thoughtfully, "it's quite likely I would strangle you."

With a sultry look perfected back when such things had been needed in her various roles, Raven murmured, "Wouldn't you rather chase me naked through the bushes?"

"Only if you run slowly and leave a trail of clothing for me to follow."

"You didn't need a trail in the Catskills."

"Was that you I was chasing? I could have sworn that was my blond harem."

"You can run, darling," Raven advised. "But you can't hide."

He couldn't run very far, either. The path he chose was, of course, a dead end. Not that either of them minded.

• • •

"What are they doing?"

On a wooded hill within the huge estate, Kelsey peered through his binoculars, then replied to the question cheerfully. "Playing in the maze." Even as he spoke, he hooked a finger under the earpiece of his headset and pulled it away from his ear. He waited until the sputterings had subsided, then replaced the earpiece and spoke again into the microphone. "Give them time, boss, they just got here a few hours ago."

"They haven't even *begun* to search?" Hagen's voice demanded.

"I have no idea. The directional mike just picked up a hodgepodge of voices while they were in the house. They might have looked before they came outside." Kelsey put his binoculars aside and sat back to contemplate the distant mansion. "Besides, it's a big house, and right now it's full of people settling in for the weekend."

"A perfect time to search."

"Luc won't forget what he's here for, boss."

"Playing in the maze," Hagen muttered. Then he sighed. "Are they still there?"

"I'm not going to look," Kelsey told him. "I'm a gentleman. Kyle says so." And he hooked his finger under the earpiece again.

Lucas found the center of the maze with no trouble, surprised at how simple it was once he'd been given the key. He saw Kyle in the gazebo as soon as he came out into the open and approached her somewhat warily. The frustrating but comical interlude out in the maze notwithstanding, he was still a bit off balance after what had happened in the trophy room.

He stepped up into the gazebo as carefully as he would have entered a dark room with which he was unfamiliar, trying and failing to read her expressionless face and serious eyes. Searching for something casual to say as he sat down on the bench beside her, he asked, "How old were you when you discovered the key?"

"Ten. Whenever we came here, I'd lose myself in the maze. My mother was appalled, of course. They would usually find me here in the gazebo, face dirty, shoes scuffed, skirt torn. I loved it out here."

He nodded, watching her. "Kyle—"

"You asked me something in the house," she said, interrupting. "The answer is that I don't know when Martin decided he wanted to marry me. He proposed for the first time two years ago."

After a moment Lucas asked, "Why didn't you answer when we were in the house? Why tell me now?"

"Maybe . . . maybe I wanted Martin to be the buffer between us," she said slowly.

"Is he?" Lucas asked in a steady voice.

"No." For the first time she reached out to him consciously, resting her hand over the strong one resting on his knee. "He could never be that. No one could ever be that."

He looked down at her slender hand, a muscle in his jaw flexing, then met her darkened eyes again. "Kyle, don't say anything you don't mean."

She smiled a little. "I won't. I don't know where we'll end up, Luc, I really don't. But I think I'm falling in love with you. I think I'm falling in love for the first time."

He went deathly pale suddenly, so suddenly that she was frightened. But before she could speak, Lucas lifted her hand to his cheek and cradled it there.

"I never knew what it meant before now," he said almost inaudibly.

"What?" she whispered.

"A reprieve from hell."

Kyle's throat was aching. She went into his arms and held him as he held her, in a fierce but passionless embrace. He hadn't let her see it, she realized. He hadn't let her see how much it meant to him until now.

Raven had been right, she thought, filled with pain. Fallen idols didn't always shatter. And sometimes they were much taller standing on solid ground.

Kyle watched him across the room, barely hearing the conversations all around her. He looked almost unnervingly formal in the black tuxedo, but the slip of red cummerbund showing just above the button of his jacket looked piratical. His silvery hair gleamed in the bright light of the huge salon, where most of the guests had gathered after dinner. His handsome face was inclined politely as he listened to the woman clutching his arm.

"That woman," Raven murmured suddenly in Kyle's ear, "is a piranha with a full set of teeth!"

Kyle sipped her drink, then said, "Uh-huh. I saw Her Highness make a dead set at Josh. What'd you say to her? The venom in the look she sent you later would have killed ten cobras."

"What I said—"

"What she said," Josh said, interrupting smoothly as he appeared beside them, "was in Spanish, thank heaven. Since Rome looked blank, I gather he doesn't understand the language."

Kyle shook her head. "He's tone-deaf and says that makes it impossible for him to speak or understand anything but English. What *did* Raven say to her?"

"You're too young to hear it." Josh looked reflective. "I'm too young, in fact."

"You speak Spanish?" Kyle asked him curiously.

"He speaks it like a native," Raven told her. "So do I. Her Highness, however, does not."

Mildly Josh said, "She claims to be a reincarnated member of the Aztec race, remember? Not necessarily Spanish in this life or familiar with the conquistadores in her previous one."

"But she understood you?" Kyle asked.

"Oh, she understood," Raven smiled gently. "It was very basic, gutter Spanish. And she responded in kind, but her retort was halting, mispronounced, and entirely too formally constructed. She's had lessons—and recently."

Josh looked up to see Lucas and Princess Zamara approaching and murmured, "Darling, please restrain yourself, all right? We don't want to get thrown out of here."

Raven slipped her arm through his and said softly, "Of course, darling. But if she starts stroking your lapel again, I'm going to draw blood."

Kyle nearly laughed, but her humor fled when she looked into malicious black eyes.

"Princess" Zamara was a woman in her early thirties—perhaps. And there seemed little question that Latin blood of some kind ran in her veins. Apart from those reasonable assumptions, any certainty about her background and intentions was pretty much a matter for speculation.

She was five-foot-nothing and teetering on six-inch spike heels to make up for the lack of height, which gave her a dandy excuse to cling to the arm of any man she could latch on to—if she needed an excuse, which quite obviously she did not. Rome's guests were dressed formally, and Zamara was showing off her best, which tonight was a glittering silver sheath with a neckline that plunged all the way to her navel and a slit up the front of the tight skirt that nearly met the neckline. Her black hair was dressed in a Gypsy-wild mass of long curls; she wore huge teardrop emeralds in her earlobes, while a third dangled between her voluptuous breasts; and silver bangles dressed each wrist in noisy profusion.

There was an earthy sexuality about the woman, an aura of animal passion that was easily noticed even by the women in the room. While the men generally seemed to be attracted in varying degrees to Zamara, every one of the women was suspicious of an accent that came and went, and a nasty feline habit of stroking male lapels.

Kyle, watching the supposed royal personage advancing toward her on Lucas's arm, examined her own feelings and found no jealousy there. And she didn't feel threatened by the other woman, except in a very basic way. She had the notion that Zamara was more dangerous to life and limb than to matters of the heart.

She hadn't had the doubtful pleasure of being introduced to the princess yet, and Kyle could see that Zamara was bent on just that. It seemed a favorite tactic of hers, clinging to a man's arm while that man introduced her to his wife or lover or friend.

Kyle winked slowly at Lucas, and the faint look of anxiety on his face eased somewhat. She was increasingly fascinated by this new version of the man, both moved and astonished to find that he was so unsure of himself right now. Whether it was the new delicacy of the bonds being forged between them or his memory of what lay behind them, Lucas was clearly concerned that no more misunderstandings or deceptions would exist between them.

But he didn't have to worry about Zamara, Kyle thought, making a mental note to tell him so as soon as possible. She felt no more threatened by the woman than Raven did, but she was aware of sensitive hairs rising on the nape of her neck. And whatever else her heritage had given her, it had also provided the blood of generations of aristocratic noblemen and women who had perfected the social art of dealing with phonies.

Lucas introduced Kyle to the princess, reaching out to take her hand and acting as if the red-tipped grasp on his other arm didn't exist. Subtlety was lost on Zamara, however. She continued to hold Lucas possessively with one hand while the other gently stroked his lapel.

"I remember you!" she told Kyle throatily, her accent no more than a faint overlay of rhythm that came and went. "You were a handmaiden at my court."

Kyle smiled, her gaze drifting to those red-tipped fingers curled over Lucas's arm. She studied the possessive hand for a fleeting moment, then looked back at Zamara's face without losing her smile. "Was I really?" she said politely. "I hope I didn't spill anything on you."

Loftily Zamara said, "Oh, no, my dear, but you were terribly clumsy. Sacrificed, of course, and such a pity. No woman should have to die a virgin."

In a very soft voice Kyle murmured something in a language that Lucas, Josh, and Raven didn't understand. But Zamara's eyes flickered. Without losing her own smile, she glanced across the room, found Martin Rome, and excused herself regally to totter off in his direction.

"What did you say to her?" Raven asked curiously.

Kyle's smile had faded as she watched the other woman move away. "Hmmm? Oh, I just said that what you miss in one life you tend to find in another."

"What language was that?" Josh asked. "It sounded familiar."

"Know any Greek tycoons?" she asked him dryly.

Lucas was gazing down at Kyle, frowning a little. "She's Greek, then?"

"I'd say so. I saw a ring like the one she was wearing in Greece, and I wanted to find out if she knew the language. She does, definitely." Kyle shook her head suddenly. "Dammit, I bet I've put her on guard."

"Maybe not," Raven said thoughtfully. "That woman would bring out the cat in a saint, and for all she knows, Greek is just your second language. She may not know she gave herself away."

Lucas looked at Josh, who shrugged and said, "I don't know, but I think they're ahead of us somehow."

"Clue us in?" Lucas requested of Kyle.

"She's just too bad to be real, Luc," Kyle told him.

"So? We figured she was a phony going in."

"I know, and we pretty much discounted her because of it. Maybe she just means to become Mrs. Martin Rome and all this overblown, mystical drama is part of it, but I think we'd better keep an eye on Her Highness. She's dangerous."

"Definitely," Raven agreed.

"All right," Josh said. "Since we planned to split up, anyway, Raven and I will keep Rome and the princess busy. You two circulate for a while, then ease out and case the joint."

"My husband, the professional thug," Raven murmured. "Darling, your language is deteriorating fast."

"I got the point across, didn't I?"

Chuckling, Lucas watched them stroll away, then looked down at Kyle. "I've gotten some very speculative looks," he offered. "Nobody's asked, but I gather they're surprised that you turned up with a man."

She stood on tiptoe to kiss him lightly, then said, "I never have before. They'll stop being surprised, though, if we—um—pull out the stops and chew the scenery."

Lucas tried to ignore his pulse's leaping response to the meaning behind her words. Carefully he said, "There's nothing I'd rather do than give in to that suggestion. I'm sure it would put any suspicions about us to rest, but I'm *not* sure it's at all wise right now."

Kyle placed her glass on the tray of a passing maid, then slid her arms around his waist and stepped closer. "Afraid of moving too fast?" she murmured, smiling.

His hands came to rest on her upper back, and the bare warmth of her flesh woke up slumbering desires with a vengeance. She was wearing a black evening gown that was strapless and practically backless, apparently held in place by her own will since it defied every law of gravity. She wore no jewelry and needed none; her hair was piled atop her head in a loose style that made her appear amazingly fragile; and her enigmatic turquoise eyes looked even deeper and more mysterious than usual.

Lucas found that his fingers were moving just a little against the silky texture of her skin, and he knew that his willpower was a breath away from disappearing completely. "Kyle, I won't have to act to make it obvious how much I want you." He kept his voice low, searching the riddle of her eyes with what had become an obsessive need. "Hell, I couldn't hide it if I had to. I just don't know how much more I can stand—and I don't want to ruin things by rushing you."

"I don't feel rushed," she said softly. "And I don't know how much more I can stand, either."

He groaned. "I wish we were somewhere else."

"We're not, though." Her smile was suddenly a whimsical expression, a fleeting bit of magic. "But it doesn't really matter, does it? Now come on. I want to introduce you to a few of these people so they'll know you aren't just something handsome I'm wearing on my arm."

His work for Long Enterprises was behind the scenes, and since much of his value to the company lay in his anonymity, Lucas wasn't accustomed to mixing socially with the wealthy, powerful circles into which both Josh and Kyle had been born. But he was as adaptable as a chameleon, and he had no difficulty in holding his own with this crowd. Instinctively he found the right responses, the correct smiles, the perfect blend of relaxed courtesy.

Only vaguely aware of his own easy charm, and almost wholly occupied with his feelings for Kyle, Lucas wasn't even conscious that he was making a good impression, and, if he had been, he wouldn't have cared. He only had eyes for Kyle, and so he missed the guardedly approving glances from many of the other guests.

For her part, and in some subtle manner that fascinated Lucas even as it inflamed him, Kyle behaved like a woman in love. There was nothing overt, no feline stroking or sultry looks such as Princess Zamara employed. Her hand rested lightly in the crook of his arm in a manner that was curiously unpossessive.

And yet, when she spoke to him, her voice was elusively lower and slightly husky. The turquoise color of her eyes looked darker, deeper. Her glances were intimate without in any way being suggestive. And though she didn't brush up against him physically, touching only his arm, she managed to make him vividly aware of her body with no more than the fluid grace of its movements.

Lucas didn't have to pretend that he was utterly beguiled and wanted her desperately. When they had circulated around the room for some minutes, he didn't have to exaggerate his intentions when he guided her smoothly out of the salon.

Kyle took the lead as soon as they were out in

the hallway, moving with some haste toward the back of the house.

"Where are you taking me?" he murmured, hoping for a room with a lock on the door. Any room.

"The library," she answered, sounding a bit distracted. "There's something I want to look for. And I think Martin's safe is in that room."

Lucas thought about that as they turned off one corridor and onto another. Then he said, "What makes you think I can open a safe?"

"Can't you?"

"Yes. But what made you think I could?"

"A hunch. Maybe I've read too many books about private investigators."

"I hope this house isn't bugged," he mused.

Kyle smothered a laugh. "No, I don't think so. But all the paintings are wired with security devices, the trophy room and library are locked tight every night, and four guards with dogs patrol outside after the house is shut up."

Lucas winced, even as he wondered how he had managed to divide his mind between his job and the powerful urge to yank Kyle into the nearest room and barricade the door. "Dogs? I hope Kelsey knows about that."

"If the house has been under surveillance, he knows. Martin doesn't make a secret of the guards."

In Lucas's divided thoughts, business suddenly took a backseat. "You look lovely tonight," he said. "Always, but especially tonight."

Kyle looked up at him as she guided him into a dark room. "Thank you," she murmured. The door closed behind them, and she heard the click of the lock. "Um . . . Luc? Shouldn't we be looking for something to help us?"

She felt his hands touch her waist and, as her eyes became accustomed to the darkness, saw the glimmer of his smile.

"Later," he murmured.

Kyle wasn't at all inclined to argue with him, but she was dimly aware that what was between them couldn't be allowed to interfere with his work a second time. She felt the smooth material of his lapels beneath her fingers, saw a flashing image of Zamara's red-tipped fingers, and somewhat defiantly slid her arms up around his neck.

Strands of his thick hair slid through her fingers like silk, and she caught her breath when he pulled her lower body against his firmly. "I—I thought you didn't want to rush things," she managed unsteadily.

"I don't." His head bent, and his lips pressed warmly against the bare flesh of her shoulder. "But I have to touch you, Kyle. I've spent so many nights . . . in the dark like this . . . remembering the softness of your skin. Remembering how your body felt against mine. Feeling your heart beating under my hand until it was my heart, and it beat so hard that it hurt."

His low, compelling voice was a caress, sliding over all her senses until she could *feel* the words, feel them flowing through her veins, tensing her muscles, weakening her bones. He was moving subtly against her, a sensual movement that made her vividly aware of the thrusting desire of his body and the aching, yielding need of her own. She couldn't breathe, couldn't draw enough air through her constricted throat to sustain life, and yet her body had never been so alive.

She felt his hand move to her side, her rib cage,

drift slowly upward over the tight silky material of her gown. And when those long fingers closed over her breast, trapping the pounding heart beneath, a rough little sound of hunger escaped the tightness of her throat. Her head tipped back as his lips burned a trail up her throat and her eyes closed, only to open a moment later when he lifted his head.

"Luc?"

Both his hands were at her waist now. He was very still, and she sensed he was trying to retain some small command over the needs of his body. And when he spoke, his voice was harsh with strain.

"When all this began, and I knew I'd see you again, I woke up one night remembering. Wondering what might have happened between us. I told myself you would have outgrown what you felt for me, but . . . oh, dear Lord, Kyle, I've made so many mistakes!"

"We both have," she whispered. The darkness of the room, she thought, left them vulnerable as they could never be in the light, and she shied away from that only because there was so little time to do what they had come here to do, and she couldn't allow a repeat of what had happened before. As important as their feelings were, a second failure to complete the job he was entrusted with could destroy Lucas.

She reached beside his shoulder to find the light switch, flicked it, and several lamps came on at once in the large room.

"We aren't going to make mistakes like those again, Luc. And we won't let the past poison the future. It's over—finished. It's behind us."

"Kyle—"

"No." She gazed up at him, her eyes direct and certain. "I won't be haunted anymore. I won't let you be. It happened a long time ago. I think we both paid, but nobody's asking us to go on paying."

"A reprieve isn't a pardon," he said finally, gruffly.

Kyle touched his cheek with gentle fingers. "I can't pardon you, Luc. I can understand and forgive—and I have. I can stop looking back and look forward. I have. Now there are only two things from the past left to deal with."

"Which are?"

"You have to do the job you were sent here to do. I think we both realize there's a danger in something similar happening again. A danger of me coming between you and your job again."

"Kyle—"

"It's true. We both know it. Not the same kind of interference, but there's still a danger."

Finally he nodded. "Yes. And the second thing?"

"That pardon you were talking about." Her voice was soft. "It isn't mine to grant, Luc. It's yours. I forgave you. Now you have to forgive yourself."

He realized then that she was right. He *hadn't* forgiven himself, had never done so, and that self-betrayal had colored his life ever since. He had hurt her, hurt himself, walked away from his responsibilities, broken the law by destroying evidence and lying to his superiors. For ten years he had lived with the knowledge that out of whatever motives he had failed badly during a critical moment in his life.

He had failed.

Gently she said, "When you asked if I wanted atonement, you were asking for yourself, weren't you? You're the one who can't forgive yourself for being human."

Lucas felt shaken, but he also felt a sense of release somewhere deep inside him. As real as the maze outside was the one within him, and ever since coming back into her life he had been feeling his way blindly, finding unexpected turns and dead ends. But she had led him to the center now, and he stood confronting his own grinding sense of failure.

Kyle wanted to turn her eyes from the wounded looked in his, but she didn't. If he could show her that naked anguish, she could find the strength not to flinch from it.

With quiet certainty she said, "It's *over*. Past. Put it behind you, Luc, and go on."

He didn't resist when she stepped back, but his hands lifted to hold her shoulders. "The worst failure," he said roughly, "was the one with you. That's the one I can't forget."

"You didn't fail with me," she told him. "I don't think I was ready then for real love. I don't think I would have known or valued what either of us had to give. Not then."

"We might have had ten years," he said.

Kyle looked reflective. "I read something once that some wise poet said. Something about the saddest words of tongue or pen being 'what might have been.' Would we have had ten years, Luc? I don't think so. If you had told me who you really were, I think I would have run from that. And if you hadn't told me, well, I would have run, anyway, eventually. I wasn't ready to love you completely. What we have now—within our reach—is so much stronger than what we would have had

then. Because we're both stronger. From triumphs
and failures and time."

"I hope you're right," he said, a bit wry but
trying for lightness.

"I know I am." She smiled at him. "But first we
have our work cut out for us this weekend: To find
the secret of this house. And this is Friday night."

He followed her lead, realizing they both needed
a little breathing space from their turbulent emotions. He felt almost exhausted, yet his body
throbbed slowly, achingly. Releasing her shoulders, he tried not to think about that. "All right.
Where's the safe? And what is it you're looking for
in here?"

Kyle turned to survey the book-lined room, frowning. "I think the safe's behind those bookshelves
by the window. There's a catch somewhere near
the third shelf. And what I'm looking for is a book
about the Rome family—and this house. A private
history printed almost a hundred years ago."

Lucas moved to the area of the room she had
indicated, his mind shifting reluctantly back to
business. "Is there such a book?" he asked, running sensitive fingers over the third shelf.

She was several feet away, scanning titles on
the shelves behind a massive oak desk. "I saw it
once, when I was a kid. Martin's wife told me all
the secrets of the house were in it. She might
have been trying to be dramatic for my benefit."

"But worth a try," he agreed.

"Got it!" They both spoke at once, Kyle straight-
ening with a leather-bound book in her hands
and Lucas stepping back to permit the outward
swing of the shelves.

And both were suddenly conscious that they'd

been locked in the room for some time. Any of the other guests, a passing servant, or Martin Rome himself could knock on the door. Kyle quickly sat down at the desk and began looking through her slender volume, while Lucas brushed up on his safecracking abilities.

A quarter of an hour later Lucas said, "He doesn't keep much here. Just a few important papers."

Kyle looked up from the book to find him frowning over a legal document that looked familiar. "His will?"

"Ummm. Dated just a month ago. Her Highness isn't mentioned, by the way."

Having returned her attention to the book, Kyle said vaguely, "He'd never leave anything to a mistress. He has a young nephew. The heir?"

"The heir indeed. If he's twenty-one or older when he inherits, the young man is to be given a private letter held by Rome's attorneys. If he's younger, the estate will be held in trust for him, until he's of age. Odd."

"What's odd about that?"

"Nothing. I mean, what's odd are the stipulations. This is more Rafferty's department than mine, but it looks as though this house and its grounds are so tied up that it would be virtually impossible to sell anytime soon. There's a paragraph here that explicitly urges the nephew and trustees not to sell. Nothing— not so much as a stick of furniture, a painting, or an umbrella stand—is excluded. And there's a complete inventory and appraisal attached to the will—dated six months ago."

She watched while he replaced the will, closed the safe, and then swung the shelves back into place. When he came over to rest a hip on the corner of the desk and gaze down at her, she said, "Well, it's unusual, I suppose. And it sounds awfully rough on the nephew. I mean, Martin has business interests, stocks, things like that, but most of his wealth is here in this house. If the nephew has to liquidate most of his inheritance just to pay taxes and keep this place intact, he could actually end up in debt."

An expression of surprise crossed Luc's face, and then one of speculation. "Maybe there's a motive in that," he mused.

"What do you mean?"

They heard laughter suddenly from the hallway as a couple passed the library door, and Lucas stood up. "Let's talk about it upstairs. I think we've been in here long enough. Will Rome miss that book, d'you think?"

"I doubt it. But I don't have any way to carry it without being obvious—"

"Let me." He took the leather-bound volume and slipped it beneath his cummerbund at the small of his back. "Come on."

When Kyle took his arm as they left the library, she wasn't even thinking about appearances. She was thinking about Lucas and about her, and hoping they could clear this assignment up quickly.

They had other things to do.

Josh studied the Rubens with a critical but wholly approving eye. "Beautiful. I'm surprised you're willing to sell it."

"It was a favorite of my father's," Martin Rome said, "but never one of mine. A matter of taste, of course." He looked at Raven. "Do you share your husband's interest?"

"This one is lovely. He has some paintings, though, that should be hung facing the wall." She looked at Josh in amusement. "All for a good cause. They're works by beginning artists."

Raven and Josh were standing with Rome and Zamara just inside Rome's gallery, a wide corridor specifically designed to display his collection of paintings. All of them noticed Lucas and Kyle emerge from a dark alcove and slip down another hallway toward the stairs.

"Those two are really something," Raven murmured softly.

"Kyle certainly fell hard," Josh agreed. "And he can't take his eyes off her."

"Or his hands," said a throaty voice.

Josh could feel Raven bristle even though she didn't lose her smile, and he somewhat hastily pulled her into the circle of his arm. "Young love," he reminded Princess Zamara mildly.

She slipped a possessive hand into the crook of Rome's arm. "*Young* love, Joshua? But isn't love at any age an exhilarating experience?"

Promptly he said, "It certainly is."

Zamara rubbed her cheek against Rome's shoulder, and before Raven's fascinated eyes the man seemed to go into a kind of stupor. He actually went a little pale, his eyes glazed over, and the hand he lifted to cover hers shook slightly.

"Excuse us," he said in a vague tone.

Raven watched them move away toward the stairs rather than the still crowded salon, then looked up at her husband. "Well, I'll say this for Her Highness—whatever she's got packs quite a wallop."

"And that's the second time since dinner they've disappeared upstairs," Josh noted.

"I hope she remembers to put both earrings back on this time. She's unnerving some of the guests who devoutly wish those two, but especially Zamara, would be a little more discreet."

"She isn't subtle, that's for sure."

"She's also trying too damned hard," Raven said broodingly. "The first time she enticed Rome upstairs, he was talking to us, remember? In fact, every time we've gotten near him, she's put in an appearance."

"Maybe she's afraid you're going to steal Rome away from her."

"Whatever her faults, darling, she isn't unobservant. I'm not terribly subtle where you're concerned, and she'd have to be blind, deaf, and stupid to think I wanted anyone else. I wonder. . ."

"What?"

"I wonder just how secure her hold on him really is. I don't think she's afraid of losing him to another woman, but she's worried about something."

"My instincts are jangling too," Josh admitted. "I feel as if we're sitting on a powder keg, and somewhere nearby, someone has lighted the fuse."

Raven nodded. "I certainly hope Lucas and Kyle found something."

Six

"It makes sense," Kyle admitted slowly, "if we accept that Martin has absolutely no scruples about protecting his family's heritage." They were back upstairs in her room. She was sitting at the foot of her bed with the Rome family book in her lap, and Lucas was leaning against a tall, burnished mahogany bedpost beside her.

"It explains a puzzle or two," Lucas said. "Like why he'd have a room full of artwork stolen if he only wanted the mask. And about his leaving the house and grounds as difficult to sell as possible. The letter of instruction to his heir is key; the nephew would have to know where to find the stuff."

"He wouldn't want to leave his heir indebted," Kyle realized, agreeing with Lucas. "But the nephew could sell off the artwork a few at a time, claiming he'd discovered them hidden, or that they were bought in good faith. He may even think that's true, and just assume his uncle wanted to protect him from inheritance taxes. The statute of limitations will likely expire before he inherits, anyway." She shook her head. "And if he *does* know and wants to avoid questions altogether, there's always the black market. Neat. As long as that stuff remains hidden, who's to know?"

"Which is why we have to find it. Or at least have some good solid evidence that the cache is here. No judge is going to issue a search warrant for Martin Rome's estate without damned good reason, and even if one did, how would they know where to look? We've been assuming he got the stuff for himself and out of a desire to look at it, which would mean he'd have reasonable access to it. If he's planning for the future, it could be anywhere. A walled-up room or closet—anything. We'd have to have a detailed and accurate floor plan of this house and then measure, inch by inch, inside and out, before we could even come close to finding a hidden vault or room."

"Daunting," Kyle observed. "It could be hidden anywhere at all. Still . . ."

"What?"

"Well, it would have been noticed if he'd had any major renovating done. Can we find out about that? Because if he didn't, then it's very likely he had to put the stuff in an existing vault some- where. A hiding place that was built years ago, maybe even when the house was first constructed. And something about it might be in this book."

"Good idea." Lucas looked at his watch. "You're not dressed for it, but it's time for our stroll in the maze. We're supposed to touch base with Kelsey at midnight, as you know. He can find out if the house has been renovated recently. My guess is that he already knows all about the history of this house."

"The northwest corner—right?"

"Right."

Kyle decided against a wrap; it was chilly outside but not really cold. She exchanged her heels for a pair of sandals, and they found it easy to slip out of the house. A full moon showed them the way clearly, and since Rome's guests were hardly the sort to chase one another through the maze—at least, not at midnight—they had the place to themselves.

The northwest corner of the maze had been selected as a meeting place with Kelsey for several reasons. It was farthest from the house, relatively difficult to stumble into by accident, and provided a dandy weak spot in the greenery where someone could push his way through.

And they found Kelsey waiting for them, his head and powerful shoulders protruding through the hedge wall, an expression of patience on his amiable face.

Lucas sighed. "Tell me something, Kelsey, would you?"

"If I can."

"How did you get into this business? You don't seem exactly cut out of the federal cloth."

"You just think so because you used to be a by-the-book cop," Kelsey told him. "Actually I'm a paragon. Now, are we just going to chat, or what?"

Aware that he'd been gently warned off the subject of Kelsey's admission into the ranks of the secretive federal agent game, Lucas became even more curious about that. But he was hardly one to pry into anyone's past after botching his own so badly, and he let it drop. Instead he explained about their search, the book and will, and the conclusions he and Kyle had reached. He ended by requesting information on possible renovations to the house.

"None," Kelsey said promptly. "Aside from a little redecoration—paint, carpeting, wallpaper and such—that place hasn't been touched in thirty years. Certainly no remodeling has been done."

"So it has to be a vault or room that's existed at least thirty years," Kyle said.

"That book you mentioned sounds like a good bet. Any luck with it so far?"

"I haven't had enough time yet to read it through," she told him.

Kelsey nodded, then looked at Lucas. "If you're planning a bit of exploring after the guests are tucked up for the night, be careful, will you? It might be best to stick to your rooms tonight, anyway. If you can't find the vault casually, then you can always skulk tomorrow night."

"It's a big house," Lucas reminded Kelsey.

"Yeah. Well, it's your show."

Lucas nodded. "We'll check in again tomorrow morning around eight; it's a reasonable time for a stroll, but I doubt any of the other guests will be up and about." He looked reflective. "This corner can't be seen from the house, can it, Kyle?"

"No. The only part of the maze that's visible from any part of the house is the roof of the gazebo."

"That's about all I can see from my spot, except for this corner and a couple of the paths," Kelsey said.

"I suppose we could send up a flare if we happened to get into trouble out here," Kyle said gravely.

Kelsey looked at her. "Not at all. Just climb up on the gazebo and start jumping up and down and waving your arms. I'll get the message."

Lucas put an arm around Kyle and said dryly, "Obviously we have a first-rate backup for this job. Let's go."

Kyle heard a chuckle from behind them and then the rustling of bushes as they walked away. "He's a strange man, isn't he?" she murmured to Lucas. "I feel like I've known him for a long time, and yet . . . well, he certainly didn't want to answer you about how he got into this business, did he?"

"So you caught that."

"You really don't know?"

"No. I've only known him a year or so, and even though he talks a lot, he doesn't say much about himself. Raven could probably tell some tales if she wanted."

"When we were back in the cabin, he said something about you."

Lucas was wary. "Oh? What?"

Softly Kyle said, "That you were very protective of those you care for and uncommonly gallant about women."

After a moment, surprised by the other man's observation and not quite sure how to respond to it, he said honestly, "Well, chivalry's the easy part of knighthood. And since I was so lousy with the rest—"

"Don't." She shivered a little but made a protesting sound when Lucas stopped and removed his jacket.

"Chivalry," he said, mocking himself lightly and placing the jacket around her bare shoulders.

"It isn't that cold," she said. "And that isn't why I felt a chill just then." She gazed up at him, her face starkly delicate in the pale moonlight. "Luc, there aren't any knights anymore. The men who slay dragons don't wear armor or ride white chargers or carry a lady's scarf into battle. They're unsung heroes," she went on softly, remembering Raven's words. "They love and hurt and bleed . . . and make mistakes. That's what makes them *real*, Luc."

They were facing each other, and Lucas was looking down at her, his face in shadow. "You're talking about that pardon again, aren't you?"

"Because we can't go back. We can't go back and fix the things we left broken. All we have is today and tomorrow."

"I know." He put an arm around her shoulders, and they began walking again. Kyle was choosing their direction since he hadn't entirely learned the maze yet, and he was surprised when they ended up at the center. "We should have gone directly back to the house."

"No, we shouldn't have." Kyle stepped up into the gazebo, pleased to find, as she remembered, that a soft, golden light was kept on at night in the little structure.

Lucas followed her, watching as she turned to face him. He felt the way he'd felt all day, unsettled, a little raw emotionally. When he saw her face, his first thought was that he didn't want to talk about this, didn't want to face this tonight.

He wanted to take Kyle into his arms and blot out the world, especially the past, just blot it out. But his second realization hit him with the force of a blow.

He knew what she was thinking.

For the first time, the very first time in their relationship, he was looking at her calm face and quiet eyes and he knew what she was thinking.

"Not tonight," he said, barely recognizing his own voice. "I don't want to talk about this anymore tonight."

"We have to. You're still tied up in knots, Luc—"

"And you aren't?"

"No. Not like you. You haven't let out the anger." He moved restlessly, hardly aware of the faint chill in the air. "Kyle—"

"Your anger at me."

"Nothing that happened was your fault."

"No? I was the cause of it, Luc. Unknowingly, yes, but I was the cause. If it hadn't been for me, you wouldn't have had to walk away from anything. That had to make you angry."

"I love you now. I loved you then."

"Because of me you had to make choices you didn't want to make." Her voice was steady. "You had to lie, destroy evidence. Your whole life was different after that. And *I* made you leave me, didn't I, Luc? If I'd been stronger, tougher, more of a woman and less a child, you wouldn't have had to go."

"That wasn't your fault," he said again, tightly.

Kyle stepped toward him. "No, it wasn't. We both know that. But you're still angry. And I won't go on with that between us."

"I'm not angry, not at you. Kyle—"

"Then why do you keep pulling away?"

He stared at her. "What are you talking about?"

"Remember back at the cabin? I got angry. The bitterness and the hurt and anger all came out. But *your* anger is still between us. We're careful and wary, and then we start to be close and you back away. The past rears its ugly head. And that wouldn't be happening, Luc, unless you were still angry. At me."

"You said you needed time," he managed.

"That isn't it and you know it. You were a stranger to me at first, but that stopped being true a week ago."

He was silent.

Kyle moved another step until she was standing before him, and her fingers were white-knuckled as she held his jacket around her. "Honesty this time, remember? And not just with each other but with ourselves. I avoided the anger and bitterness ten years ago, but I've faced them this time. You lived with it then, maybe buried it somewhere, but you haven't faced it, not really. Now you have to."

After a moment he leaned against one of the white Doric columns supporting the roof and sighed raggedly. This was harder, much harder, than facing his own failure. This felt like a betrayal. "I love you," he said simply.

She wasn't going to let him avoid it, not this time. "But you were angry—when you left me and in the years since."

"I didn't want to be angry." His low voice was strained, hurting. "I loved you, and you were so . . . so fragile. I stood there that night, looking down at you while you slept with that suitcase open on the floor by my feet. Moonlight was shining on the bed, on you, and you looked so damned fragile. I knew I'd have to leave you."

"And you were angry at me," she insisted softly, "because the drugs were there. Because you'd seen me get that case. Because you had to leave."

"Yes," he breathed finally. "I wanted to stay with you so badly, and I was so angry that I was shaking. I kept telling myself to wake you up and confront you, find out for sure about the drugs, but I couldn't. I didn't want to see the light in your eyes go out when I told you who and what I really was. Anything seemed better than that. Even—"

She quietly finished for him when his voice broke off. "Even leaving me."

His hands found her shoulders, and he was aware that beneath the thick fabric of his dinner jacket were the delicate bones of her body, the fragility. The deceptive fragility.

"It wasn't right to blame you," he said roughly. "I knew it. I *knew* it. But I did blame you. For a while. I don't blame you now, Kyle, and I haven't for years. I read all the articles about you in the newspapers and magazines, and I nearly went crazy thinking of you being hurt in one of those dangerous stunts you kept pulling. And I couldn't be angry anymore. Don't you understand? Anger never had a chance."

Kyle reached up to touch his cheek lightly with her fingertips. "Then stop pulling away from me," she whispered. "Being cautious. Stop being worried that one of us is going to make a mistake this time."

He knew that was true, knew that caution had

indeed held him back. And his voice was raspy when he said, "Tonight you look so *fragile*! The way you did that night . . ."

"That night was a long time ago," she said, her arms sliding up around his neck, her fingers twining in his hair. "This is *now*—and I'm not fragile now, Luc. Not like that. I'm strong enough to love you now, strong enough to love the man you really are. Will you deny me that?"

He caught his breath when she moved even closer, pressing her warm and yielding body against him until his own body throbbed in a heated, aching rush of desire. And the same surge of primitive emotions that he had felt in the trophy room enveloped him again, driving out everything but the essential need to feel her body alive in passion, hear her voice husky with it, and see her eyes nakedly wanting.

"Kyle . . ."

His lips found her parted ones, fierce and demanding, a demand she responded to with instant fire. For the first time they kissed with nothing hidden, nothing holding them back. And everything that had come before was only a pale preview, a ghostly hint of the sheer, raw emotion to come.

Kyle trembled violently, dazed by the feelings capturing her body. She was hot, cold, weak, strong, ravenous. Ten years of remembering a single night had not prepared her for this explosion, this eruption of all her senses. Her body was no longer her own; it was his, bonded to him, linked to his in some magical, overpowering affinity. And the hunger for his possession was alive in her, hurting her with its need.

Lucas drew back at last, staring down at her with darkened eyes, his breath raspy in the quiet of the night. Without a word he slipped an arm around her shoulders and guided them both out of the gazebo and into the maze. And it was Luc who found the way out, even though he was hardly conscious of it.

Neither of them noticed that his dinner jacket lay on the floor of the gazebo, the crumpled remains of formal distance.

Guests still laughed and moved around the mansion, but Kyle and Lucas hardly saw them. They went into the house and up the stairs, perfectly paced, and no one who looked at them could doubt that they were in a world of their own.

Kyle's room was closest, and they found it awaiting them with welcome, the bed turned down and the lamps softly lighting the room. That faint golden light enabled Lucas to see what was in her face when she turned to him beside the bed, and it almost stopped his heart.

"I love you," she whispered.

He framed her face in his hands, gazing into her turquoise eyes and seeing the naked wanting there. And seeing the love, astonished, awed, an unstoppable force. "I love you," he told her with soft intensity. "I've always loved you."

Kyle could feel the burning of her body's need for him, the aching emptiness, and she wondered, with a sudden instinctive fear, if she really could let go with him and be as free as she had been on that other night so long ago, if her feelings could fully escape the prison where they had remained all these years. "I—I'm afraid," she murmured. "It's been so long. . . ."

"Shhh." He kissed one corner of her trembling mouth, then the other, gentle. "I'm afraid too," he confessed.

"You?" She was surprised, moved. "Why?"

"Ten years of memories," he said with a crooked smile. "I'm afraid I won't please you, love. Afraid the shattered pieces of that god of yours will cut the both of us."

His vulnerability gave Kyle the courage she needed, and her hands slid slowly up his chest to unfasten his tie. The buttons of his white shirt parted, one by one, and the golden flesh of his chest was hard and roughened with springy hair beneath her seeking touch. "You'll please me," she whispered. "We'll please each other."

She could feel his big, hard body tremble, feel the unsteadiness of his hands when one slid down her neck and the other searched out the side zipper of her dress. His mouth found hers, tender at first but instantly heated. And she could only dig her fingers into his shoulders, hold on urgently as that unfamiliar, frightening explosion consumed her senses.

But she wasn't about to ruin this night by being afraid. She loved Lucas, and that was what mattered. All that mattered. Willfully she loosed the floodwaters of her own emotions a second time, holding nothing of herself back. Love and need, fierce desire and aching tenderness, a jumble of feelings flooded over her and through her. And fear, never very strong, was swept away in the powerful current.

She gasped when his lips left hers, and her head fell back to allow the hot exploration of his mouth. She felt the zipper of her dress give way, felt the silky slide of material as the dress fell to pool around her feet in darkness. Her sandals were easily discarded, the dress kicked aside. His fingers nimbly found the pins in her hair, sending them flying so that her hair fell down around her shoulders. And she twined her fingers in his hair, trembling when his mouth slid lower.

He pressed kisses in a lingering trail between her full, aching breasts, down the taut flesh of her rib cage and quivering belly. His fingers gently drew the last scrap of lace and silk down her long legs.

Kyle was lost in some heated, dizzying place, blind and deaf to everything but him, his touch. She was hardly conscious of being lifted, until she felt the softness of the bed beneath her back, wondering vaguely when he had stripped the covers farther back. Not that it mattered. Dazed and yearning, she lay waiting while he rapidly, carelessly, discarded his clothing.

He was beautiful, she saw, beautiful and proud and strong. Golden flesh reflected the lamplight as his muscles rippled with every movement, and she quivered just looking at him. Had she seen that ten years ago? No. She had only seen then with a young girl's fascination in a body so different from her own. Now she saw the hard planes and angles, the utterly male sculpting of flesh and bone and muscle that caused her breath to catch.

Desire was an ache, an intolerable emptiness housed within her burning body, and the soft sound that escaped her when he joined her on the bed was husky and hurting.

His feverish gaze moved slowly over her, and Lucas groaned softly. "You're so lovely, Kyle. . . . "

He kissed her deeply, his tongue possessing, twining with hers in a passionate joining, a preliminary possession that seared them both. His hand moved lightly over her breastbone, lower, seeking and finding the thrusting curve of her breast. A rosy nipple was hard to his touch, and she moaned when he tugged gently. His lips followed the satiny slope, caressing flushed skin and then capturing the rosy bud hungrily.

Kyle couldn't breathe, couldn't be still, as pleasure made every muscle in her body grow tense. She caught at his shoulders, compulsively stroked his smooth, golden skin. Despite the differences brought about during ten years apart, this was the body she knew, the body she craved, and the need to touch him was helplessly overwhelming. She said his name over and over in her mind, unable to say it aloud, unable to make any sound at all except for the husky, kittenlike whispers of desire.

Her legs parted at his gentle, insistent touch, and Kyle abandoned herself completely to sensation. The empty ache inside her grew, swelling in throbbing surges. The shatteringly erotic caress of his fingers, the swirling rasp of his tongue at her breast maddened her, pulled at her until hunger was all she knew, all she was.

She had never known that such feelings were possible. He had been gentle and careful ten years ago, so much so that her memories of that night were filled with that tenderness, that care of her. But she had been too young, too inexperienced to feel the complete range of sensations a woman's body could know. She had found pleasure in his arms, but nothing had prepared her for what he was making her feel now.

"Luc . . ." It was a whisper, ragged, urgent. She thought she'd go crazy if he didn't take her now, make her his again.

Lucas could feel his own passion building, his body aching as he forced control. She was unimaginably lovely, and he was mesmerized by the changes maturity had wrought in her body. Dizzily he thought of a flower just budding, then a flower in full, glorious bloom. Parted from her so long ago, he had not been able to watch that lovely transition; he could only remember then and see her now.

Then slender and fragile, virginal yet so utterly giving, so passionately fiery in his arms. And now still slender but with the ripe curves of womanhood igniting his senses, no longer virginal but still new to this physical loving and still so utterly responsive and giving.

Ten long years . . . And impossible to forget that, impossible to forget how long he had ached for her.

How long he had loved her.

The hoarse little sounds she made drove him wilder, and her shaking hands on his shoulders, his back, seared his nerve endings. Her breast throbbed beneath his lips, and the slick heat of her need beckoned irresistibly. She was starkly beautiful in passion, fierce and strong and exciting. She was ten years of dreams. He thought he'd explode with wanting her and knew he would never, ever, get enough of her.

"Luc . . ." The almost inaudible, husky sound of his name on her lips was an invitation, a de-

mand, a plea, and he responded with driven eager-
ness. Her trembling legs parted for him, welcom-
ing him, and the silk of her inner thighs against
his hips was the touch of home.

She was gazing up at him, her clouded eyes
fixed on his face, wondering, needing.

"I love you," he whispered in a rasping sound,
and his body joined with hers in a movement so
smooth and certain, it was as if time itself had
decreed it, sanctioned it.

Kyle caught her breath, her nails biting into his
shoulders. She hadn't remembered. Dear God, she
hadn't remembered how it really felt. Her body
accepted his, but she could feel the taut stretching of tissues that had known a man's possession
only once so long ago. And there was a brief,
instinctively fearful moment when he felt alien
inside her, an intruder that would steal something from her. But then it was all right, it was
perfect, and her body was responding wildly to
the throbbing fullness it had captured.

Lucas had half closed his eyes, still and trembling
in that hovering moment of waiting. His chest
moved with every harsh breath, and control was
something he clutched desperately when the mol-
ten tightness of her body sheathed his.

"Kyle?" A whispered question.

And it was Kyle who moved first, her body arch-
ing into his, the instinctive undulations of her
hips beginning the dance both their bodies craved.

Lucas groaned, and his body responded to the
invitation of hers. The burning of his need tor-
tured him, and he couldn't get enough of her,
couldn't satisfy the imperative necessity of meld-
ing them into one flesh, one being. It seemed that

his body demanded compensation for the long years apart from her, demanded a possession so complete, so utterly absolute, that she would always be a part of him.

And it seemed that Kyle craved the same thing. She was wildness incarnate, demanding with a woman's desperate, instinctive drive toward completion. Her body loved his, fought his, captured his totally. With every breathless, raw sound she held him; with every touch of her hands she seduced him; with every taut tremor of her body she humbled him.

Control was a distant thought splintered by need, an unimportant thing neither wanted or needed. Frenzied necessity held them captive, spurred them on. It was a kind of madness, impatient, driven, aching wildly, far beyond their dominion.

Kyle thought she would certainly go mad and didn't care. The tension of her need was torture; sweet, raw agony. She was breaking, tearing. Her heart was pounding out of control, her breathing raspy, and primitive sounds tangled in the back of her throat. And then, in a mind-numbing instant, she was shattered, pieces of herself flying away into oblivion, and she held on to Lucas's body as the center of reality in a world gone mad with pleasure.

The exploding ecstasy that Kyle was experiencing captured Luc, held him fiercely, and he cried out, even as she did, the hot, inner contractions of her body driving him to the edge and then over it, making him intensely alive, killing him, changing him forever. . . .

He was heavy, and she gloried in that male

strength. She felt dazed, shaky, and yet tension was building again. While aftershocks of that incredibly sensual earthquake still shook them, she could feel the rise of desire in them both.

Lucas rolled slowly, carrying her with him, his lips seeking hers blindly. Their feverish bodies clung together, merged still, and he kissed her as if only the sharpest edge of hunger had been blunted.

Her breath lost again, her self lost again, Kyle responded eagerly. And in the hours that followed, she was conscious only of delight. Like lovers with very old souls long ago committed to each another, they made love again. In aching need, as if the morning would tear them apart forever, they made love.

Desire drove them until each touch and kiss sensitized their flesh almost unbearably, until the featherlike brush of fingers and lips was like a torch branding raw nerves. Until even the meeting of eyes was unbearable and yet was borne; almost agony and yet they craved it.

Insatiable, they loved. In the lamplit quiet of the room there were only faint sounds. Beloved names whispered, soft vows, simple, private words of need. And the low, raw sounds of anguished release, of aching pleasure.

And though two hearts and minds would have worn the night away in love, their earthly selves finally yielded to exhaustion. Bodies entwined, limbs tangled, utterly limp, they slept.

Kyle woke slowly, and in the first disoriented moment it seemed that ten years had not passed at all. For an instant she was that seventeen-year-old girl, her first night of love behind her—waking to the shocking absence of her lover.

She didn't want to open her eyes; she wanted just to lie close beside Lucas under the warmth of covers he must have drawn up over them. She wanted just to lie there and feel what she should have felt then: warmth and love and incredible happiness.

And in that moment the last faint throb of that old wound signaled the final healing.

She felt him move slightly and opened her eyes, gazing up at him as he lay propped on an elbow watching her.

"Hello," he said softly.

Kyle could feel the delight of her own smile. "Hello." She studied his face in fascination, learning it all over again. And she had never known, never guessed, that so hard and masculine a face could look so tender.

He lowered his head and kissed her slowly, thoroughly, and Kyle felt an instant, hot tremor.

"I love you," she whispered when she could.

Lucas smiled at her, and his eyes were dark. Huskily he said, "When I left you before, I knew that one day I'd find you again. Crawl to you on my knees if I had to. I used to wake in the middle of the night, thinking you were with me, beside me. But you never were. Until last night. Kyle, I love you so much."

Kyle touched his cheek, her eyes misty, and her voice was shaking. "You said something last night about the pieces of that broken god cutting us both. But it never broke, Luc. Not then, not since. It's just standing on solid ground now . . . and it's taller than it was before. No pedestal, no glittering image, just a man I love with all my heart."

A rough sound escaped him and he kissed her again. "I don't deserve you," he said almost inaudibly. "But I'll spend the rest of my life trying to, love. If you'll let me."

She went very still, her breath caught somewhere near her heart. "Luc?"

He cupped her cheek with one big, warm hand. "You asked what would happen on Monday. I only know what I want to happen. Marry me, Kyle. Be with me always."

"There's no place I'd rather be," she whispered, and went into his arms again.

Seven

The necessity of reporting in and pangs of hunger finally drove them from their room just after seven. They found that the huge staff of the mansion had cleaned up after the night before and had even had a buffet breakfast ready at this early hour. But other than themselves and the staff, no one seemed to be stirring yet.

By eight they were in the maze, and Kyle left Lucas to report in with Kelsey while she went to the center to find his dinner jacket. The jacket was lying over the low railing of the gazebo, and just inside the little structure was Martin Rome.

"You're up early," he called as she approached.

Kyle, never easily embarrassed, stepped up into the gazebo and picked up Luc's jacket. "I love mornings. And I had to get Luc's jacket."

Rome glanced at the jacket, then studied her face. Conversationally, as if he were discussing something only mildly interesting, he said, "A serious love affair for you, obviously."

"Very serious," she confirmed.

He leaned against a column; he was dressed, as she was, in slacks and a thick sweater, and he was as wide-awake as she. Suddenly Kyle was on her guard. She wasn't quite sure why, except that there was something in his dark eyes she had never seen before. And this had nothing to do with Lucas's mission here; this, she knew, was strictly between the two of them.

"I'm willing to overlook it," he said finally.

"Gracious of you," she said dryly. "But I'm not asking you to overlook anything, Martin. I love Luc."

Rome was clearly amused. "Of course you do, my dear. I'm sure he's been breaking hearts for years. But would you really wish to share your life with an ex-policeman, fired in disgrace years ago?"

Kyle stiffened.

He was still smiling. "Outrage, Kyle? Why? Because I had your lover's background checked out? I considered it my responsibility, to your father as well as to myself. Despite your pretty fabrications, Kendrick is nothing more than a former cop, disgraced ten years ago and living ever since on the bounty of various wealthy women like you."

Kyle managed to work up even more outrage; it wasn't difficult. "I don't care what you say about Luc," she told Rome in a low, shaking voice. "It doesn't change my feelings—or his. And you had no right to look into his past, no right at all!"

"As your future husband, my dear—"

"I'm not going to marry you! I told you that two years ago, and I've repeated it since."

"Then your father will disinherit you," Rome said calmly.

She stared at him, honestly astonished that he thought that would sway her. "I don't care."

"I imagine Kendrick will care."

Kyle didn't want Rome to begin speculating on why Lucas in fact, would not care, so she didn't defend that point. Instead she tried to place herself in the unfamiliar position of a rich young woman who just might have been betrayed in her choice of lover.

Raising her chin and trying to feel like the spoiled, selfish society darling that Rome obviously believed her to be, she said, "He won't care, either. He loves me!"

"I'm sure he's a very proficient lover," Rome agreed blandly.

It took all the control Kyle could muster to keep herself from leaping at him, enraged by his casual dismissal of what she and Luc had shared. But she forced herself to remember everything that was at stake. "How dare you!" she bit out stiffly.

In a tone of faint reproof, and as if she had not spoken at all, he said, "Once we are married, my dear, I will expect an heir before you begin taking lovers. A man must be certain of his heirs, and I assure you I will be very sure of mine. Discreetly you may take all the lovers you wish—afterward, of course."

Kyle couldn't believe the conversation, simply could not believe that the man was serious. She held Lucas's jacket tightly, trying to work up a little righteous indignation. "So that's the kind of marriage you've planned, Martin? And I suppose your future wife, may the Lord help her, would be expected to turn a blind eye to your reincarnated Aztec *princess*?"

"Zamara is no threat to you," he said indifferently. "A mistress is entirely apart from a wife."

"*She* wants to be your wife," Kyle told him. Giddily she thought, Divide and conquer! Maybe if she could encourage a little dissention between Rome and his mistress . . .

For the first time he looked just a bit startled. "Nonsense. Zamara is perfectly aware of my intention to marry you."

Since Josh and Raven had not been alone in noticing Zamara's effect on Rome, Kyle decided to use her own observations to good effect. "Martin, you have got to be out of your mind. You're putty in her hands and she knows it. And if you think any sane woman would marry you with your little princess standing by, you'd better do some more thinking. It won't happen."

He stared at her, frowning. "Then I shall send her away."

"Right." Kyle gave him a tight, disbelieving smile. "You can't do it. She only has to touch you. Everyone noticed, Martin. I wasn't the only one."

"I am in control," he told her flatly.

Kyle just stared at him scornfully.

And, quickly, Rome was back in control of himself. "You will marry me, Kyle. Your family expects it. Whether or not I choose to have a mistress is none of your concern."

Distantly Kyle said to him, "Luc is meeting me here in a few minutes."

He studied her for a moment and then shrugged. "I see I shall have to let this little affair of yours run its course. But you might consider being honest with yourself and telling Kendrick you'll be disinherited if you marry him. Then watch how quickly he drops you, Kyle."

Kyle gazed after him for long moments, then sank down on the bench behind her.

From an upstairs window in the mansion, Zamara looked down on the maze. She could see the gazebo and, just barely, a couple of feet of green grass around it. She had seen Martin go into the gazebo, as he often did. She had seen Kyle Griffon go into the gazebo. Later—too much later—she had seen Martin leave the structure.

Zamara tapped her long, scarlet-tipped nails against the glass, frowning. The fool! Couldn't he see that the woman was in love with her blond lover, and he with her? Zamara had excellent instincts when it came to adventurers, being one herself, and she was certain Lucas Kendrick wouldn't have cared if Kyle Griffon lost every penny she had.

Glancing back over her shoulder, Zamara looked at the tumbled bed with less than her usual satisfaction. Martin was thoroughly under her spell; she would bet on it. Indeed, she did bet on it. Yet he was still determined to marry his blue-blooded Kyle.

It was a troubling situation. Zamara carefully weighed the attractions of Kendrick against the power of a few million dollars and came up with an unequal balance. Abandoning everything for a lover was found between the covers of some child's story, never in real life. With money and power a woman could buy all the lovers she wanted; without either, she was likely to find herself thrown over for a younger, prettier, and wealthier woman somewhere down the line.

Zamara went to her closet and threw open the doors, then began rapidly changing from her silk nightgown. Something had to be done, and quickly. Martin was too bullheaded to give up Kyle, and she just might be persuaded to give in to him.

It had to be stopped.

"Something is bothering you," Josh murmured, kissing his wife's bare shoulder. "You should still be asleep."

Raven didn't protest when he pulled her over on top of him, just folded her arms over his chest and smiled down at him. "So should you. I read somewhere that men in their thirties begin losing stamina."

"Is that a pointed reference?" he asked, wounded.

"I was just thinking they should have used you in that study. You would have messed up their curve."

He chuckled softly. "Actually it's all due to my beautiful wife. I just can't seem to get enough of her."

Raven traced his smiling lips with a finger, then kissed them. "Good," she murmured.

"Now tell me what's bothering you," he urged quietly.

She grimaced. "Can I fall back on woman's intuition?" she asked.

"I won't object," he told her. "But I'm willing to bet it's more along the lines of a good ex-agent's experience and instincts. Anything concrete?"

"No. No, but I feel we're missing something that

could be important. Something about Rome. He just seems a little . . . well, off center. And did you notice how he was watching Kyle last night?"

"I noticed. But Luc said something about his having proposed to Kyle a while back. Could that be it?"

Raven was struggling silently to bring her instincts about people into focus. "He looked at her as if she were one of those trophies of his. He wasn't jealous of Luc; he didn't even seem to take any notice of him. And except when Her Highness had her claws into him, he watched Kyle all the time she was in the room."

"And so?"

"Well, there was something implacable in his eyes." Raven shook her head. "Dammit, I just can't get a fix on it. But I've an awful feeling that there'll be some kind of confrontation before we all get out of here—and it won't have very much to do with that stolen art."

Josh couldn't add to that, but he took serious notice of Raven's anxiety. She had excellent instincts, years of experience in dealing with complex people, and he respected her very, very much. And since Lucas was one of his best friends, and Kyle was growing steadily in his estimation, he wanted neither of them to get hurt in any way.

"It's Luc's show," he said slowly.

Raven chewed on her lower lip. "I know. We should talk to him and Kyle first. But—"

"Reinforcements?"

"We're batting a thousand so far," Raven said. "I'd hate to blow the average by losing one of us."

It was a sobering thought. They *had* been relatively charmed since Hagen had first drafted them.

But they were playing some potentially very rough games, and the law of averages was against them.

"Kyle?"

She had had only a few minutes in which to decide how much to tell Lucas. And it wasn't a question of lying to him or even of holding back information she was perfectly willing to share with him; she was just concerned that Rome's fixation on her could interfere with Luc's work here. In the end it was because of his work that she decided to tell him what had happened. He needed to have all available information, period.

"Did you tear Kelsey away from his coffee again?" she asked, smiling as Lucas sat down beside her.

"Field rations this time, he said. And he didn't sound too upset about it. What's happened?"

"Martin was here," she said readily.

"He upset you." Lucas's facial muscles tightened. "Why?"

Deliberately lightening the moment, she said, "He called you a gigolo."

After an instant Lucas's tension eased and he smiled. "He must have pulled quite a few strings to get that on a weekend. So he *did* check into my background."

"He certainly did. And he couldn't wait to tell me you were disgraced, drummed out of the police force, and have been earning a living these last ten years by being nice to rich women."

Lucas shook his head. "I'll say this for Hagen: When he plants information, he does a swell job. Rome bought it?"

"Oh, yes. It's something he understands very

well." Kyle lifted a brow at her love. "Good thing you warned me about that false trail."

"You can ask Josh," Lucas said, gravely but with a twinkle.

Kyle smiled at him, and her turquoise eyes were alight. "I'd believe you if you told me the earth was flat, darling."

"Oh, damn, I was saving that for later as a test." But his eyes were alight, too, and his kiss was warm and tender. Then he studied her face. "There's something more. What else did Rome say?"

She looked down at the dinner jacket in her lap, smoothing the material with her fingers. Lucas wasn't going to like this. "He intends to marry me, Luc. He even made a threat, and he sounded pretty sure of himself."

"What threat?"

Kyle wondered vaguely if Lucas could possibly know just how menacing his low, compelling voice could become under certain circumstances. Like these. Keeping her own voice casual, she said, "He told me that my family expected me to marry him and that I'd be disinherited if I didn't." She glanced aside and saw that his face was expressionless.

"Would your father do that?"

Kyle considered the question. "It's possible, maybe even likely. Even though he doesn't take much interest in me, I've noticed that he found quite a few opportunities for me to see Martin these last years. He hasn't said anything to me directly, but he completely approves of Martin. And blackmail would be just his style—to tidy up my life all in the good name of our family, you understand."

Lucas was silent for so long that she looked at him anxiously. "Luc? For all intents and purposes, I was disinherited years ago. It doesn't bother me, and I wouldn't have married Martin in any case. Surely you realize that?"

He hugged her swiftly. "Of course I realize it, love. It's just that I don't want to be the cause of a final break with your family."

Serious, she gazed at him. "My parents' lack of interest in me has hurt more than once, but nothing will change that now. The final break came a long time ago, Luc. For years I thought that it wasn't natural not to love my parents—but that's past. I'm grateful to them for giving me what they did, but I don't want anything they can offer now. I just want you."

Huskily he said, "You've got me, love." He kissed her, both of them aware of a swift rise of desire. "I think this gazebo's bewitched," he added a bit more hoarsely.

Kyle smiled at him. "I cast a spell on it when I was a kid," she told him gravely. "This was my magic place, remember? The place where dreams took wing."

He chuckled softly. "Your spells last a long time, I see."

"Bet on it," she whispered, kissing him.

"Eight-thirty in the morning," a deep male voice said somewhat dryly.

Without taking his eyes from Kyle's upturned face, Lucas said, "Go away, Josh."

"No," his employer said politely. "I've come to discuss strategy, whether you like it or not. And to tell you, Kyle, that Her Highness has been looking for you, and Raven thinks you three would do better alone."

Looking reluctantly at the other man, Lucas said, "Do better at what?"

"Finding out where the princess stands in all this," Josh told him, sitting down on the bench across from them and stretching his long legs out comfortably. He was holding a mug of steaming coffee in one hand, contemplating it thoughtfully. "She's probably right too. And we need to know, Luc."

Kyle got to her feet. "Yes, we do need to know." She looked at Josh. "Strategy?"

He returned her look, his cool blue eyes warming a bit. "Raven feels a storm coming, and she's usually right about things like that."

Kyle frowned a little.

"Ask her about it," Josh invited. "Maybe you two can put your heads together and figure out our host."

Remembering the peculiar expression in Rome's curious, dark eyes, Kyle decided that might be best. She was uneasy about him, very uneasy. "Right." She leaned over to kiss Lucas. "See you later."

He watched her disappear, still holding his jacket, then looked at Josh with pained eyes.

Smiling, Josh saluted him gently with his coffee mug. "Now you know how I felt after I met Raven. These bloody assignments of Hagen's do get in the way, don't they?"

Lucas's only answer was a heavy sigh.

Kyle found Raven first, since the other woman

had come out onto the terrace looking for her. They both sat on the low stone wall, far enough from the house so that they couldn't be overheard if they spoke in low voices, which they did.

"Zamara wants me?" Kyle asked.

"That's what she said. She's at the buffet at the moment, but we heard her ask two maids if they'd seen you. Think she wants to have it out with you?"

"About Martin? I don't know. He said that she knew he intended to marry me."

"Intended?" Raven lifted a flying brow. "Sounds like the man's made up his mind."

"Sickening, isn't it?" Kyle shook her head. "I lightened it a bit when I told Luc, but Martin even tried blackmail. Threatened me with dis-inheritance."

"Can he do that?"

"My father can, and he probably would." She grinned faintly. "I just realized. If we find that stuff, and Martin is arrested, Father will certainly reexamine this perfect match of his. He might even be persuaded to see Luc in the light of savior of the family name. Scandal rubs off, you know, especially if you stand too close to it."

Raven smiled at her. "So, no more fairy tales?"

"The real thing," Kyle said, "is a lot better." She looked at the other woman, whom she felt so close to now. "Want to be my matron of honor?"

"I'd love to," Raven said promptly.

"Good. Unfortunately we have to get through this weekend first. What's this about you feeling a storm coming?"

"Rome. And since you've told me about his *intentions*, I'm feeling even more alarm. Were you supposed to be blind to Her Highness, by the way?"

"A mistress would be none of my concern, if you please."

"Bastard," Raven said without heat.

"Yes, medieval. He honestly didn't know, though, that Zamara had some pretty permanent intentions of her own."

Raven pursed her lips and gazed into space. "First his apparent belief in this reincarnation business, which he openly admitted to last night after you left the room. Then his obvious sexual reaction to Her Highness, which is just a bit too excessive for him to reasonably believe she's only a mistress. And then his intention to marry you, even if he has to use blackmail. I don't like it. Not one bit."

"Oh, listen to what Luc and I found out." She quickly told Raven about the will and book, and about their deductions regarding Rome's apparent desire to preserve his family treasures by using the stolen artwork.

And Raven didn't like that, either. But before she could comment, Her Highness found them.

"Ah, Miss Griffon." She looked pointedly at Raven. "If you will excuse us?"

Raven smiled gently. "I'll stay. Surely you don't mind?"

Zamara weighed her for a moment, then shrugged. "As you please. Perhaps, though, Miss Griffon would prefer to keep this discussion between herself and me."

"Not at all," Kyle said politely.

Black eyes flashed at them both. "Very well,

then. My dear, you really should take your man and leave."

Kyle studied her thoughtfully. "Oh? And why is that?"

Zamara laughed with careful lightness. "Because Martin has the absurd idea that he can persuade you to marry him. Nonsense, of course, but men are sometimes silly."

Raven was gazing critically at the toes of her boots.

Kyle smiled faintly. "Yes, they are. Still, I wouldn't worry if I were you. I don't want Martin, and you certainly seem to have him in thrall."

Raven coughed and looked even more intently at her boots.

Her voice growing even sweeter, Zamara said, "He is a very determined man, my dear, and determined men are dangerous once they've set their minds on something—or someone. And, for your information, Martin won't leave my bed until *I* say. Wife or mistress, I will control him."

"Then why worry?" Kyle asked practically.

"I would prefer wife. With you gone, that's what I'll be."

After a moment Kyle said, not without sympathy, "I could give him an heir. You couldn't. Is that it?"

Zamara stiffened. There was a flash of something in her eyes and then, abruptly, she looked more natural than either of the two women had seen her before. "You're right. I can't have children."

Kyle nodded. "I see. Well, you really don't have to worry about me. I'm in love, Zamara. Martin could offer me the earth and it wouldn't make any difference. Luc and I will be leaving first thing Monday morning. As planned."

Zamara nodded suddenly. "Yes, I see. You really do love your man. It happens. I'll trust you."

"Thank you," Kyle said gravely.

A glint of wicked humor shone in Zamara's eyes. "There are ways of holding a man to your side, my dear. And since I'll never have a daughter . . ." She leaned forward and whispered softly in a startled Kyle's ear.

Raven, glancing sideways, saw her friend's eyes widen.

Then, with a laugh and an almost automatic look of spite at Raven, Zamara swept into the house.

"Good heavens," Kyle said faintly.

Raven was laughing, curious. "What?"

Kyle cleared her throat. "Umm . . . ask me again sometime, huh? I think I just found out why Martin goes into a daze when she touches him."

"That's one secret," Raven said definitely, "I'm not about to let you keep to yourself."

Kyle giggled. "Later, all right? I have to make sure it works first." Then she burst out laughing in earnest.

"He could be here in a few hours," Josh said neutrally.

Leaning back against the railing of the gazebo, Lucas frowned. "I know. I wonder if it's necessary, though. We're getting jumpy, maybe that's all it is. We have to find that mask, the cache—or both. Nothing says there has to be trouble."

"But if there is trouble? Kelsey's damned good,

we both know that. Zach would be insurance. We couldn't risk coming in here with guns and walkie-talkies, so we really don't *have* insurance. And if we're going to search the house tonight, we may well need all the help we can get."

"Guards patrol after the house is locked up," Lucas noted.

"Yes. He'll slip in before."

Lucas sighed explosively. "I want it to be *over*. I want that bastard behind bars. The way he looks at Kyle isn't normal. I could understand if he loved her, but I don't think he feels any emotion for her at all. He just—thinks. Cold-bloodedly."

"Raven said something along those lines. It's worrying her."

"It's worrying me too. Kyle made light of it, but I think he scared her out here a little while ago. He told her she'd marry him, then threatened her with disinheritance."

Josh whistled softly. "Ruthless."

"I'll say."

Calmly Josh said, "Her father won't do that, you know."

Lucas looked at him curiously. "Kyle thinks he will."

Smiling a little, Josh said, "No. He's of the old guard: Family first and damn everybody else. Disinherit his only child? Terrible scandal. He'd put a good face on it if she married the butler."

Lucas grinned a little. "Well, she's marrying me. One step *below* the butler."

"Don't be ridiculous," Josh said. "You're going to save his daughter from the consequences of Rome's folly. You might even get a smile out of him. Congratulations, by the way."

"Thanks."

"Shall we go and find our ladies before they give in to their instincts and scratch Zamara's eyes out?"

"I suppose it would be bad form to let them."

"Not cricket at all."

Kelsey sat back and put his binoculars aside. "Lot of meetings going on down there," he reported into his microphone.

"Meetings between whom?" Hagen asked ominously.

"Kyle and Rome. Kyle and Luc. Josh and Luc. Raven and Kyle. Raven, Kyle, and Zamara." He paused to reflect for a moment. "You know, they just don't act like agents." He put the earpiece back in place when the sputtering had subsided.

"Is anybody *working*?" Hagen asked.

"Beats the hell out of me. Luc reported in a little while ago, nothing new. Except those fences. Mended, I'd say."

There was a moment of silence, then Hagen grasped his meaning. "Kendrick and Miss Griffon?"

"Uh-huh. They have that look."

Hagen sighed. "When does Kendrick check in again?"

"After lunch. We're all right unless Rome wonders why there's so much activity in the maze. I suppose he'll put it down to young love, though."

"Are they *planning* to work?"

"The plan is to search the house tonight. I don't know, though, boss. It's a pretty slim chance. Big house."

"It's all we've got. Build a fire under them."

"They'll do what they can. You know that."

"Yes. Report in when you've talked to Kendrick again."

"Aye, aye."

Kelsey put the headset aside, then picked up the binoculars again and looked at the house. He focused on an upper window, frowning.

Martin Rome was looking down on the terrace where Raven and Kyle sat talking.

Being a good host, Martin Rome had available numerous activities to save his guests from possible boredom. There were horses on the estate. Tennis. A heated pool. Even a small golf course.

Lucas, Kyle, Josh, and Raven went riding, deciding that they might as well go on being a foursome. Several other guests went along, which prevented private discussions.

Lunch was a drawn-out affair with all guests attending, and it was well into the afternoon before Lucas and Kyle could slip away to the maze again for their check-in with Kelsey.

What he had to tell them sent them back to the house in a sober frame of mind. They found a private moment to report to Josh and Raven, sobering them as well.

"He couldn't have heard anything," Kyle mused as the four of them stood alone in the trophy room.

Raven bit a knuckle thoughtfully. "Maybe he didn't have to. Just seeing us with Her Highness may have unsettled him. We have to assume so, anyway, and be on guard."

Josh looked at Lucas and raised a quizzical brow. "Zach?"

"I think so. Just in case."

Raven laughed softly. "Good. I'm curious to see if Teddy comes along."

Lucas sighed as the other two went to use the phone in their bedroom. "Just as well, I suppose. When this gang gets together, things usually happen."

Taking advantage of the moments alone, Kyle slid her arms around his waist. "What's this about Teddy coming along?"

"Zach will try to keep her out of this," Lucas explained. "He doesn't want her in his kind of jungle."

Kyle thought about that. "You mean because of the danger?"

"Yes. Zach was born to it. Danger, I mean. And it's against his very nature to allow someone he loves to follow the same trails. He's probably pacing like a caged cat right now because he isn't here watching over Josh. And me."

"Will Teddy come along?"

"Oh, yes."

Curiously she said, "You sound certain."

"I am. Teddy is the only person I've ever known who can make Zach act against his own nature anytime she wants. Josh can do it sometimes— but not all the time."

She smiled up at him. "You're all very close, aren't you?"

"Well, we've been together for years, and in some pretty sticky situations from time to time." He thought about their relationships, realizing that Kyle wanted to understand, and trying to frame a good explanation. "I guess Josh is our—pivot. And not because he's the boss. He knows things about all of us that he keeps to himself. For instance, I know he hasn't told anyone but Raven about that favor he did for me ten years ago."

"He helped you through that time, didn't he?"

Lucas brushed a strand of hair back from her face, his fingers lingering to touch her cheek. "Yes, he did. He didn't ask questions, but he listened when I got drunk one night." He grinned a little. "He even got drunk along with me. Now that's friendship."

Kyle smiled up at him. "I'm glad he was there for you."

"So am I. If he hadn't steadied me then, God knows what I would have done." Lucas drew a deep breath. "And now I've got you, love."

"You certainly have," she murmured.

Eight

Kyle managed to study the Rome family book several times during the day, disappointed not to find some clue as to where Rome might have hidden the artwork. She found plenty of information, most of it slanted to show the family in a good light no matter what; she found the Rome crest, which was an elaborately ornate *R* set within a series of double-lined boxes; she even found a motto, or rather a little jingle that one of Martin's ancestors must have penned and had included in the book.

But nothing about a hidden room or vault.

It was important to Kyle that Lucas's work here be completed successfully. She believed it was the last remnant of the past that needed to be settled.

But by the time for dinner came that night, they still had come no closer to having any idea where to look. Lucas slipped out to the maze to report a final time to Kelsey that they had no choice but to search tonight, returning to tell the others that Zach and his new wife had indeed arrived. Between them they had decided where best to slip the new arrivals into the house and when.

All they needed was a sleeping household.

The party dragged on. Kyle was at first relieved that Zamara had redoubled her efforts to keep Rome ensnared, staying with him constantly and keeping her hands off other women's men. But as the night wore on, she began to be uneasy. And she wasn't the only one.

"Look at him," Raven murmured at one point. "His eyes are glassy. She's got him right on the edge."

"But on the edge of what?" Lucas responded softly. He drew Kyle a bit nearer to his side, worried because that glassy stare occasionally wandered in her direction.

Josh was studying the older man across the room, and his expression was a bit grim. "I don't know, but I don't like it. I think it'd be best for all concerned if we get this job wrapped up tonight."

"You won't get an argument from me." Luc checked his watch. "Midnight. The party's breaking up quickly. Zach and Teddy should be waiting."

"Meet you in your room," Josh murmured, and guided his wife off into the dwindling crowd.

Lucas and Kyle also drifted off, leaving the room with the absorbed expressions of lovers with private things to do on their minds. They worked their way toward the far end of the house, moving more quickly when they'd left the guests behind, and slipped down several deserted hallways before entering a small room. It was a parlor-type room, formal, and with the air of being little used. French doors opened out onto the second of the three terraces, this one constructed with a view of the rose garden.

"We can get upstairs to our room from here without being seen?" Lucas asked.

"Servants stairs behind that door over there. They go all the way to the top floor, and there's a landing almost across from our room."

"Childhood exploration?" he asked.

Kyle smiled. "Hide-and-seek, when I really didn't want to be found. It was one of my favorite games. Luc, I know this house pretty well, and I can't remember a sign of a hidden room or vault. I was a child, of course, but if it was here, I should have found it years ago."

He nodded. "I know. But we're running out of options. It's the only game we've got."

Lucas locked the door leading out into the hallway, and Kyle went to ease open the French doors. She had to open them wider a moment later, amused because no one had thought to tell her that Zach was so big.

Well over six feet of big. He had broad, powerful shoulders which the black of his sweatshirt did nothing to diminish, and it was obvious he had muscles to spare. And no one had to tell Kyle he was a dangerous man. It wasn't that he tended to fill doorways; it wasn't even that a wicked scar twisted whitely down his lean cheek. What it was about the man that would frighten even the stout-hearted was a palpable aura of leashed power and an atmosphere of cold menace.

He moved like a big cat as he came into the room, as if he walked on dried leaves and wished to be silent. And he would have been silent even with dried leaves underfoot. The dark clothing he wore did absolutely nothing to conceal the danger of him, nor did the calm, almost bland expression on his rugged face or the serene gray eyes.

Born for danger, indeed, Kyle thought.

On the big man's heels came his new wife, a petite woman somewhere in her twenties with an unruly and beautiful mass of red hair, and the big, soft brown eyes of a doe. She looked delicate and fragile, but her small face was vividly alive, and Kyle thought there was a great deal of strength and spirit beneath that dainty exterior.

Quick introductions were made, and then Kyle was leading them into the stairwell while Lucas unlocked the hallway door and joined them. They found the stairs clear and were soon safely inside Kyle's room.

"Where's Josh?" Zach asked immediately, his voice soft and effortless.

"Downstairs," Lucas reported, loosening his tie. "He and Raven will be up soon."

Zach made himself comfortable in a large chair, pulling his wife down into his lap and giving her a look that was a somewhat comical mixture of adoration and annoyance.

"Don't fuss," she told him severely in a musical voice. "I'm here, and that's that."

He grunted. "I know, dammit."

Lucas went to change into clothing more suitable for skulking, while Kyle softly and rapidly filled the new arrivals in on their progress to date.

Zach nodded when she was finished, then gestured to the walkie-talkie he had set on a table by the chair. "Kelsey has the other. He's on watch and in touch with Hagen." He studied Kyle, his gray eyes intent. "You say Rome's acting strangely?"

Kyle sat down on the foot of the bed and sighed. "You could cut his tension with a knife. It may only be Zamara's weird control over him, but we've all decided that the sooner we're out of here, the better."

After a moment Zach said, "I checked out his family. His nephew—you said he was the current heir?"

"According to his will, yes."

"An interesting young man," Zach murmured.

"In what way?" Luc asked as he returned to the room wearing dark slacks and a black turtleneck.

Zach's mild, heavy-lidded eyes continued to study Kyle thoughtfully. "I suppose a polite way to put it is that he's careless with money. And he's recently incurred some whopping gambling debts. Big-time bookies. I'd say the young man has the beginning of a serious gambling problem."

Kyle looked at Luc as he sat down beside her. "Maybe that's why Martin's so determined to marry me; he wants another heir. Zamara knows it. And if he's becoming consciously aware of the sexual hold she has on him—"

"He could be obsessed by now," Luc finished grimly. "Dammit, Kyle, I wish you were out of here. If she keeps pulling him toward her while he's obsessed with marrying you, he may snap."

"He's never been known to lose his cool," Zach noted. "Never emotional or violent. But if that kind of pressure's building up in him now, he may lose it completely."

"You armed?" Lucas asked him.

"Ankle holster." Zach nodded toward the small duffel bag he had brought along. "And a few extra."

Lucas went over to kneel and check the guns Zach had brought, and it was Kyle who went to answer the soft knock at the door. Slipping quickly into the room, Josh and Raven were also dressed in comfortable dark slacks and sweaters. And Josh spoke instantly to Teddy.

"You're always in his lap," he said dryly.

"That's where he puts me," she replied, unembarrassed and somewhat amused.

"Zach, did you bring my gun?" Raven was asking, going to peer over Lucas's shoulder.

A little bemused, Kyle gathered up her clothes and went to change in Luc's room. Intrigued by all of Luc's friends just hearing about them, she was completely fascinated now after seeing them together. Between them all there was an easy familiarity, a kind of camaraderie that struck her as being very rare. They've been through more than one fire together, she thought.

And Kyle herself felt accepted into that closeness, something that both delighted and moved her. She had known few friendships in her life, and to be so readily accepted into Lucas's circle of friends was something she treasured.

The future looked bright indeed.

If they could only get through this night.

She returned to her bedroom to join the others, who were lounging comfortably and talking in low voices. The guns had been distributed, with Lucas, Josh, and Raven all carrying theirs at the small of their backs beneath concealing sweaters. Teddy, like Zach, wore an ankle holster. Kyle readily accepted the automatic Lucas handed her, pleased to discover that these men—even with Lucas's gallantry and Zach's clearly protective nature—treated the women in their life as capable equals.

"I read you'd become a sharpshooter," Lucas told her with a smile.

Kyle checked her gun and put it inside the waistband of her pants at the small of her back, returning his smile. "Did you? Well, it's nice to know those supermarket rags are good for something."

He chuckled. "Actually it was *People* magazine. That competition you won in California."

"I'd forgotten about that."

He shook his head, then looked at Josh where the other man rested a hip on the low dresser. "How many guests were still downstairs when you left?"

"Just a few. And from the look of things, Her Highness plans to keep Rome fully occupied once they get upstairs."

"Let's hope she's successful," Raven murmured.

Lucas nodded, then said, "We'll split up into teams. Zach, you and Teddy take the ground floor. Josh and Raven can take the second floor, and Kyle and I will take this one."

"Just how legal is this?" Kyle wanted to know.

"Not very," Josh told her, amused. "If Zach and Teddy are found here, they could be charged with breaking and entering by Rome. The rest of us are here by invitation, but we were hardly invited to search the house. Caught, we'd look damned suspicious. Still, if we find the mask or the other stuff, it'll be enough to get the police in here legally with a warrant. We're okay with the guns, since we're all licensed to carry—"

"I'm not," Kyle said, interrupting.

"Yes, you are," Zach told her. "I have the permit if anyone asks."

She stared at him. "You think of everything."

Solemnly Teddy said, "He's well versed in the art of skullduggery."

"I resent that on Josh's behalf," Zach said mildly.

"Leave me out of this," Josh requested. "Everybody knows I'm a model citizen."

Kyle looked at him, rakish and rather dangerous in his dark clothing, and giggled suddenly.

Raven grinned at her. "I know. I haven't decided if they're commandos at heart or ten-year-olds."

"Look who's talking," Josh said chidingly.

It was as if none of them carried guns or waited to search a house in the dead of night, Kyle thought, as if no danger surrounded them. They were six friends talking casually.

And she believed she knew then why Hagen had drafted these people and cannily made use of their talents.

He would have been a fool not to.

The house was silent when they slipped from the room and went their separate ways. There were occasional lamps to softly light their way, and each carried a small flashlight, courtesy of Zach's well-equipped duffel bag.

It was a big house. Moving silently and whispering when they needed to, Kyle and Lucas searched carefully. Of course, the bedrooms were off limits due to sleeping guests, but there were many other rooms. Salons, sitting rooms, innumerable closets and storage areas, alcoves and pantries. And it was a slow business because they had to check every possibility and be utterly silent all the while.

With at least half their floor covered, Kyle became aware that there was something bothering her, an idea at the back of her mind, and gradually realized that a passage she had read in the Rome family book was nudging her.

"I want to take another look at that book," she whispered. "I think I missed something."

Lucas was examining a closet full of linens and spared a moment to glance worriedly at her. "Be careful, will you, love?"

She stood on tiptoe to kiss his cheek. "I'll just be in our room. Back in a flash." She disappeared around a shadowy corner of the hallway.

Lucas gazed after her for a moment, then glanced at his watch and went back to work. It would be dawn in another hour; they were running out of time.

In their darkened bedroom, Kyle found the book and carried it to the window, making use of moonlight as she flipped through the pages. Something . . . what was it? She stood holding the book, her abstracted gaze focused out the window. Then she frowned and looked down at the book again. Slowly her finger traced the Rome family crest engraved on the first page. An ornate *R* surrounded by a series of double-lined boxes.

With fingers that trembled in sudden excitement, she turned the page to the verse written by one of the Rome ancestors. This time she read it carefully.

An artist's eye can picture

*A lover's heart can feel
But few are those so certain
That dreams can become real.*

*You may find love in Paris
Even share the wealth of Rome
But you never truly hold it
Till you touch the golden dome.*

Kyle raised her eyes slowly and stared through the window. She could see the dark shape of the maze and, at its center, bathed in moonlight, the dome of the gazebo. The golden lighting inside it, remaining on during the dark hours, made the shape of the little structure glow warmly.

"The golden dome," she whispered. That had to be it. The Rome crest was an initial within a maze, and that had to be where "the wealth of Rome" could be touched.

Rome's hidden vault wasn't in the house at all—it was secreted somewhere in, or beneath, the gazebo!

On the point of rushing out to tell Lucas, Kyle hesitated. What if she was wrong? They'd waste time out there if both of them went. But if she searched hurriedly first . . . After all, who knew that gazebo better than herself?

And Rome.

Kyle bit her lip in an instant's indecision, then set the book aside and hurried from the room. Raven glided from the shadows on the second-floor landing to look at her quizzically.

"I want to check the gazebo," Kyle whispered without pausing.

Raven frowned after her for a moment, then turned back to find Josh.

Kyle hadn't forgotten the guards and dogs outside but trusted her ability to get across the terrace and into the maze without rousing them. She waited at the terrace doors for a few moments, watching the two guards pass each other outside. She allowed them a few more moments, than slipped outside silently.

She reached the maze without being detected and moved swiftly along the familiar paths, undisturbed by the smotheringly tall, dark hedges, by the stark shadows of moonlight.

The gazebo, softly lighted, welcomed her to the center of the maze, and she stepped up into it. Now . . . where? She studied the structure slowly, carefully. There was no ceiling; the rafters supporting the domed roof were exposed and painted white. The Doric columns were slender, each decorated with an ornate *R*; the floor apparently solid. The benches had thin padding and spindly legs.

It had to be the floor.

And there had to be a switch of some kind. Kyle turned in a slow circle, then began probing the columns and railing with delicate hands.

Josh and Raven found Lucas on the third floor, coming out of Kyle's room, a strained expression on his face. "Have you seen her?" he asked them in a whisper.

"She said she was going to check the gazebo," Raven answered softly. "I think she has a pretty good idea there may be a hiding place out there."

Lucas swore softly. "She shouldn't be—"

Zach and Teddy moved quietly down the hall

toward them. "Somebody crossed the terrace a minute ago," Zach told them. "A man."

The walkie-talkie hanging at his side whispered softly.

From his vantage point on the hill, Kelsey watched the house constantly. He swore irritably when he realized that the setting moon was stealing his light, but he could still make out the house pretty clearly. He methodically studied each window on each floor, checked the whereabouts of the guards, and sent the lighted gazebo a glance.

Then he stiffened. "Something's going on down there," he reported softly into the microphone.

"What is it?" Hagen asked.

"Don't know. Somebody moving—damn this angle!" He adjusted the binoculars and leaned a bit sideways. "It's Kyle. She's searching the gazebo."

"What?"

"Wait a minute. I can just barely see her. That's what she's doing, though." He caught a glimpse of something else then, a small, darkly shining object in the hand of someone else in the center of the maze.

Swearing, Kelsey reached for the walkie-talkie.

"Looking for something, my dear?"

Kyle turned slowly, holding her face expressionless with effort. The first thing she saw was a wicked black revolver held in a steady hand. Martin Rome's hand. And when she looked at his face as he stepped up into the gazebo, she felt cold clear through to her bones.

His face was still, calm. But there was a faint twitch at the corner of his right eye, and the eyes themselves were unnaturally brilliant. Mocking.

"I—I dropped a ring," she said finally.

"I'll buy you another," he told her soothingly.

Very conscious of the weight of her automatic at the small of her back, Kyle made no attempt to reach for it. It was her ace, all she had, and a last resort.

"I don't want a ring from you, Martin. I don't want anything at all from you." She was trying desperately to keep her voice even and calm.

"Since we're going to be married," he told her in that same ominously soft tone, "I'll show you my secret. As the mother of my son, it'll be your right."

Kyle swallowed hard. "Martin, why do you have a gun? You're frightening me."

"I'm sorry, my dear, but I really can't allow your lover to steal my treasures. That is what he's after, you know. He was searching in the house. You weren't with him, of course. I knew you wouldn't be. I knew you'd be here. This is where the newest of my treasures belongs. I'll keep you here for a while, and then he'll go away."

"No," she said softly. "He won't."

"Of course he will. Then you and I will be married, and you shall provide me with an heir. My nephew Phillip is no good, I've realized that; he doesn't deserve to have my treasures. But our son will."

"Marry Zamara," Kyle urged, stalling for time.

"She's barren," Rome told her. His jaw tightened. "Pity. I would have married her otherwise. She is descended from my people in a sense. But I was able to obtain her medical history and so discovered the truth. She really should have told me herself. I can't approve of deception."

Chilled, Kyle wondered how to reason with a madman.

He looked at her seriously. "I will make you happy, my dear, I assure you."

"What of Zamara?" Kyle whispered.

His jaw tightened again. "She will go."

Kyle didn't dare push that; she could see the tug of war in his face, the awful conflict. Steadily she said, "I'm going to marry Luc, Martin."

"He won't be able to find you," Rome said reasonably. His free hand reached into the pocket of his jacket and produced a key. Stepping to one side, he reached out and inserted the key into the ornate *R* on one of the columns; Kyle had found that keyhole only a moment before he had first spoken.

Pinned in place by the brilliant dark eyes that never left her, by the gun that never wavered, Kyle was helpless.

Rome turned the key, and instantly there was a soft grinding noise. The entire gazebo moved, sliding smoothly to one side. "My grandfather had it constructed," he told her pleasantly. "I've updated the wiring, of course, years ago. It's a perfect place to store my treasures, isn't it, my dear?"

Kyle looked down at the step of the gazebo, which now led to more steps and a dark cavity in the ground. "I'm not going down there," she said tightly.

Rome smiled. "You will, you know. Or shall I go into the house and kill your lover?"

"*Rome!*"

Instinctively Kyle threw herself to one side, even as Rome whirled and fired his gun. The blast was hideously loud, followed instantly by the distant barking of the guard dogs and, seconds later, by another shot.

Rome, teetering on the brink of the steps, clasped his wounded hand with a cry as his gun clattered to the floor of the gazebo. Losing his balance, he pitched forward, down the steps and into the darkness.

Lucas, his face white, vaulted over the low railing of the gazebo and gathered Kyle into his arms. "Are you all right?" he asked in a rasping voice.

Kyle was aware of other voices, of running feet and the shouting of the guards, but her entire attention was only for him. "I'm fine," she whispered. Then, lifting her face from his throat, she stared at him fiercely. "What took you so long?"

Equally fierce, he said, "Next time, dammit, tell me what you're planning to do!"

A sudden gurgle of laughter escaped her, and Kyle threw her arms around his neck. "Next time," she promised serenely.

The sun was well up. Kept from the maze by federal marshals, Martin Rome's guests milled around in the house, confused and curious. Inside the maze, more marshals made trips into and out of the vault, carrying priceless gems, paintings, and other artwork out so that they could be inventoried.

A rotund little man supervised the activity, pausing for only a moment to tell Zach and Teddy, "You aren't here."

"Of course not," Zach said calmly.

Hagen nodded, then looked somewhat sternly at the other four, who were relaxing in the gazebo. "We're going to have to discuss the statements you give," he said.

Lazily Josh asked, "What's to discuss? We're just guests here. Rome, maddened by jealousy, decided to kidnap Kyle at gunpoint. Luc missed his fiancée, came looking, and was just in time to stop Rome. He's licensed to carry a concealed weapon. Mind you, we have no earthly idea why Rome kept all these paintings and things under his gazebo. But it's a good thing Luc got here before Rome could lock Kyle in with them."

Hagen looked at him narrowly for a moment, then nodded. "And you'll so testify?"

"Luc will, of course. And Kyle. The rest of us have nothing to say. We were just drawn out here by the commotion."

"Excellent." Hagen went back to his supervising, looking like a gleeful cherub.

"Josh—"

"It's time for you to go public, Luc. With the investigative staff you've built over the years, there really isn't a need for you to stay behind the scenes."

Politely Lucas said, "And I suppose it never occurred to you that by testifying I'll make headlines? Headlines that Kyle's father will no doubt read?"

Josh frowned. "No, that never occurred to me."

Lucas said something rude.

Kyle chuckled. "I love it." She looked at her future husband with a smile. "And that shot of yours was really something—hitting his gun hand!"

"Nerves of steel," Josh murmured.

Lucas glared at him. "My nerves were shot to hell and gone, and you know it! It was a lucky shot, that's all." He listened to their laughter with a pained look, then beckoned Kelsey over.

"You want something, hero?"

"Kelsey, we've all had a long night. Don't push it."

Grinning, Kelsey said, "Right. Did you want to tell me something else?"

"The mask."

"It isn't with this stuff."

"I know." Finding himself the focus of startled eyes, Lucas added somewhat bitterly, "We've been staring at the damned thing ever since we got here."

"Where is it?" Kyle asked.

"Come on and I'll show you." Lucas led the way from the maze, holding Kyle's hand firmly. They were followed by Josh and Raven, Zach and Teddy, and Kelsey and Hagen.

"I love a parade," Kelsey murmured to himself.

Once past the milling crowd of guests, Lucas went into the trophy room, halting before a wall with a display of numerous African tribal masks.

Looking up at the wall, Kyle asked incredulously, "You mean he hung it on the *wall* right out in front of everybody?"

"Why not? None of us caught it."

"You did," she reminded him.

"Yeah, but only at the last minute. After you left me last night, I started wondering about the mask. It was a symbol of power, so it stood to reason Rome would keep it nearby—and *it* was something he'd certainly want to look at. It wasn't likely he would have put it with the stuff he meant to keep totally hidden. So it had to be here."

"Which is it?" Josh asked.

Zach, the only one of them who had seen a picture of the mask, gestured. "Try the one in the middle."

Lucas lifted it down, and all of them saw. The mask had been covered with a dark adhesive material to closely match its fellows, but the back shone pure gold.

Nine

Kyle stood gazing out at the Pacific Ocean, smiling to herself. She loved this place. The house perched on its Oregon cliff as if it belonged there, and it was a wonderful place to spend a honeymoon. She looked down at the golden band on her finger, and her smile became even happier.

Strong arms slipped around her from behind, and Lucas rested his chin atop his wife's head. "It's still early," he murmured. "I thought you would have gone back to sleep after I went to answer the phone."

"What did Josh have to say?" she asked.

Lucas chuckled. "Nothing, really. He just said it wouldn't be right if our honeymoon wasn't interrupted by something. Rafferty and Sarah are the only ones who've managed so far to be left completely alone."

"That's why he called?"

"That's why. Remember I told you we interrupted

his honeymoon because of that problem on Kadeira? I really think he's getting even for that."

Kyle laughed.

He smiled at the sound. "Do you feel better now that Rome will be getting the treatment he needs?"

"Much better. I couldn't help but feel sorry for him, especially when Her Highness breezed past him while the paramedics were working on his hand."

"You mean her parting words?"

"Well," Kyle said fairly, " 'Ciao, baby' seemed just a little coldhearted."

"I'll say." Luc reflected. "It's a good thing the marshals weren't won over by her tricks. She might not have been involved with the theft of that artwork, but she sure as hell encouraged Rome to get that mask."

"Thinking it would help bind him to her," Kyle agreed. "It backfired on her, though. She had him so convinced he was descended from a great and ancient line of rulers that he decided to preserve his 'treasures' and family name no matter what the cost. And he'd become so paranoid about protecting those treasures that she was losing all control over him."

"Did you hear what she screamed at the marshals before they dragged her out?" Luc asked.

"Saying that she'd tried to persuade Martin not to get the artwork? Yes, I heard. Interesting language, huh? She was probably telling the truth. As far as she was concerned, Martin was wealthy enough; she wasn't worried about future generations. And keeping the artwork on his estate probably shook her even more. She knew very well the search was on for that stuff and likely knew he was under suspicion."

"I'd say she had good instincts," Lucas agreed gravely.

Her smile widened. "Well, anyway, it was nice of Martin to break down and confess so we wouldn't have to stick around for the trial and testify. Our statements made a big enough splash in the newspapers."

"Big enough for your father to notice, anyway. Did I hear him apologize to you at the wedding?"

"You did. Surprisingly enough."

Lucas turned her around gently and gazed down at her. He heard, in her steady voice, the sound of a child who had wanted affection so desperately for so many years—and had received none at all. "Give it time, love. Maybe they'll never change. But maybe they will."

Kyle slipped her arms up around his neck, smiling. "I know. It isn't so important to me now, Luc. You've given me so much more than I ever expected."

"I love you," he murmured, kissing her with tenderness and a slowly building need.

Somewhere between the window and the bed, their robes fell away, and golden morning sunlight followed them warmly.

Feeling so incredibly loved and wanted, Kyle smiled at her man. Her lips parted beneath his, turquoise eyes only half open, beautifully dreamy as they looked into his own. The need to touch him was a constant one, and she obeyed her needs willingly. Her hands molded his shoulders, traced his spine slowly, feathered along his ribs. One silken leg moved slowly to brush his hip in a smooth, tingling caress.

He lifted his head at last, breathing harshly,

their gazes locked in a rising fire. He felt one of her hands slide over his chest, the other along his ribs. Her lips were swollen, beautifully red and trembling, her breasts lifting and falling quickly with her shallow breaths. She was looking at him, he realized, moved, as if he were everything she had ever wanted out of life, everything she had ever dreamed of.

And no fantasies of godlike men were reflected in her beautiful eyes this time. No glittering gold dust. No shaky pedestal. Just a deep and enduring love for the man she had chosen.

He knew then that he would have gone through those ten numbing years again if he could have been promised the look in her eyes now. Everything—the pain and self-doubt, the bitterness and anger, the loneliness—every ragged emotion he had felt in a decade was worth this.

"Luc, I love you."

The feelings inside him were almost too much to bear, fierce and sharp and wild. And as much as his heart felt, his desire drove his body. He willed control, finding it a struggle as always but needing to luxuriate in this because he could never get enough of her, because he loved her and needed her so much. His hands moved to shape rounded flesh, his mouth surrounding the hard, throbbing tip of her breast. Her soft whimper of pleasure sharply increased his own, but Lucas found a thread of control and hung on fiercely.

He traced the valley between her breasts with his lips, moving slowly downward over the quivering flesh of her stomach. His tongue dipped hotly into her navel, and he felt a stronger quiver shake her, heard a faint sound from her. He slid his

hands along her slender legs, rubbing slowly over
the satiny skin, fascinated by the feeling of her
warm body, finally moving back up along her hips
and under them. He kissed the sensitive hollows
above each leg.

He could feel the restless heat of her and murmured something low in his throat, soothing, his
fingers seeking the slick, hot center of her desire.
Kyle moaned softly when he found it, sending
shock waves all through her, and her body twisted
in a sudden, helpless reaction.

She could feel his lips touching her thighs, caressing, moving ever closer to the tormenting
fingers. Her legs trembled, and there was a mol-
ten heat in the pit of her belly, burning her, bring-
ing her so vividly alive that she ached all over. She
wanted to scream, to let out some wild cry of need
and pleasure and agony. And she did cry out,
softly, when she felt his lips touch the ache. She
cried out wordlessly, her nerves splintering, all
her breath leaving her for an instant in a gasp.

She felt that wonderfully familiar feeling, as if
she were stretched tightly, about to break into
pieces, her heart pounding against her ribs with
thuds she could feel strongly. All her conscious-
ness seemed to focus on him, on what he was
doing to her, and if she could have found words
and forced them out, she would have asked him
why he was doing this, why he was tormenting
her this way.

But she could find no voice, no words, and the
plea in her mind was a desperate, growing agony.
Her head moved restlessly on the pillow, and her
breathing was shallow, ragged. Primitive little
sounds came from her throat, tangled and hurt-

ing. She didn't think she could stand it; her entire body rebelled against the torture, twisting, and her heart was choking her with its fierce pounding.

He moved finally, rising above her with a taut face and blazing eyes, every muscle rigid and quivering. Kissing her deeply, he whispered hoarse words of love into her mouth.

His own control broke into splinters, and his body joined hers in a sudden thrust. Kyle cried out, her eyes widening, conscious of nothing but the sheer pleasure of him deep within her. There was an emptiness now filled, and the ache in her was partially satisfied. She cradled his body, her limbs moving to enclose him, feeling the strength and power of him, feeling her heart and his pounding together.

Kyle could feel her body reaching, stretching mindlessly for something almost beyond reach. But it was there and she knew it, knew Luc could take her somewhere glorious. And she clung to him, murmuring a plea she didn't hear, the emptiness in her filling . . . filling . . . bursting suddenly in a mind-splintering explosion of sensations far beyond pleasure. Her entire body shook, heat searing her flesh and her soul, and her cry was a breathless sound of exaltation.

Lucas groaned harshly when her body contracted around him, his own body surging toward release. He buried himself in her, the white-hot strain of his need giving way suddenly in a burst of sheer ecstasy.

Lying drowsily at his side, Kyle suddenly remembered Zamara's advice on how to hold a man.

Grinning a little, she decided it couldn't hurt to try it. Knowledge like that shouldn't go to waste; it would be criminal. And why shouldn't she try it? Later, maybe. When she had the strength to move.

"What are you smiling about, love?" he murmured.

"Oh, nothing." And there was nothing *wrong* with it, after all. Seducing a much beloved and loving husband. Nothing wrong with it at all.

Lucas raised his head and studied her smile. "When did you turn into the Mona Lisa?"

"I don't know what you're talking about." But she could feel the smile.

"That smile." He showed her a look of mock uneasiness. "Now I know why that smile fascinates people. It's three parts evil, dammit."

"You're imagining things."

"I am not. You're up to something, wife. I know you are. What are you up to?"

"Not a single thing, darling."

But she was, of course. And late that night, after a candlelight dinner and a seductive nightie that didn't have much chance to seduce before it wound up on the floor, she let him know just what she was up to.

"Three parts evil," he managed in a drained, somewhat dazed voice long into the night.

"I'll have to thank Her Highness."

She had to explain, of course.

Later.

Epilogue

Kelsey gave his boss a wary look as he came into the office. "You wanted to see me?"

"I have an assignment for you, my boy," Hagen told him briskly.

Making himself comfortable in the visitor's chair, Kelsey frowned. "I don't know, boss. You've gotten too damned good at matchmaking lately for my taste. I'm nowhere near ready to get married."

Hagen stared at him, wounded. "Do you really believe I would deliberately lose my best agent?"

"Deliberate," Kelsey said, "has little to do with the matter. You've hit more bull's-eyes by accident than on purpose."

"It won't happen again," Hagen said definitely.

"Let's not take any chances," Kelsey begged. "No female partner this time, all right? Don't send me to a tropical island, or to the back of beyond, or to a secluded estate, or even to a large city. I think that covers it."

Hagen stared at him.

"I'm not ready to get married," Kelsey repeated firmly.

"You'll be working with Derek this time."

Kelsey blinked. "Derek? Your outlaw Derek? The man who never believes a single, solitary thing you tell him? The man who doesn't use guns? That Derek?"

"That Derek."

After a moment Kelsey said slowly, "Must be some job if you've roped him into it."

"It is, indeed. And we know almost nothing about what's going on. You two will be on your own."

Kelsey cursed his curiosity.

But he sat forward to listen.

THE EDITOR'S CORNER

February is a favorite LOVESWEPT month. After all, it's the month dedicated to love and romance—and that's what we're all about! Romance is (and should be!) more important in our lives than just one special day, so LOVESWEPT is claiming February as a whole month dedicated to love. What a wonderful world it would be if we could convince everyone!

In this special month, we have six marvelous books with very pretty covers. In our LOVESWEPT Valentine month we have given all of our books covers in pink/red/purple shades—from pale pink confection, to hot fuschia pink, to red-hot-red, and passionate purple. This is our way of celebrating the month—so be sure to look for the SHADES OF LOVESWEPT covers, and we know you'll enjoy all the stories inside.

Our first book for the month, **STIFF COMPETITION**, LOVESWEPT #234, by Doris Parmett, is a heart-warming and very funny story about next door neighbors who are determined not to fall in love! Both Stacy and Kipp have been burned before and they go to ridiculous lengths to maintain their single status! But he can't resist the adorable vixen next door and she can't stop thinking of the devil-may-care hero of her dreams. When Kipp finally takes her in his arms, their resistance is swept away by sizzling passion and feel-
(continued)

ings telling them both that it's safe to trust again.

TOO HOT TO HANDLE, LOVESWEPT #235—This title tells all! Sandra Chastain's new book is full of sexy flirting, outrageous propositions, and hot pursuit. Matt Holland is a man after Callie Carmichael's classic convertible—or is it her cuddly, freckled body? Callie's not interested in any city slickers like Matt because she's a country girl living a free and easy life. But his kisses are too wonderful and they are bound to change her mind . . . and her lifestyle!

Next we have **SHARING SECRETS,** LOVESWEPT #236, by Barbara Boswell. We first met Rad Ramsey and Erin Brady in an earlier Barbara Boswell book, **PLAYING HARD TO GET,** which was a story about their siblings. Now Barbara has decided that Rad and Erin deserve a book of their own—and we agree! Sexy heartbreaker Rad knew women found him irresistible, but he'd always enjoyed the chase too much to keep the ladies whose hearts he captured. Erin had never known the fiery thrill of seduction, but Rad's touch awakened a woman who would be satisfied with nothing less. When they found each other, Rad knew he couldn't ignore his feelings and Erin knew she wanted this powerful, sensual, and loving man. This is a provocative story of a woman's first real passion and a man's true love.

Those incredible men surrounding Josh Logan are just fascinating, aren't they? Kay Hooper gives us another of the wonderful romances in what Carolyn Nichols calls the "Hagan Strikes Again Series" next month with **UNMASKING KELSEY,** LOVESWEPT #237. There is a terrible aura of fear hanging over the sleepy little town of Pinnacle, and beautiful Elizabeth Conner figures prominently in an episode that brings Kelsey there on the run and brings danger to a boil. Elizabeth also figures prominently in Kelsey's every thought, every dream . . . and she finds him utterly irresistible. This is one of Kay's most gripping and sensual romances and it seems to have "Don't You Dare Miss Me!" stamped all over it!

There's no more appealing Valentine story than
(continued)

MIDSUMMER SORCERY by Joan Elliott Pickart, Love-swept #238, an unforgettable story of first love—re-newed. Fletcher McGill was back in town after six years and Nancy Forest was still furious at the man who captured her heart and then deserted her. They've been lonely difficult years and now Nancy is determined that Fletcher feel the full force of her hot anger—but instead, desire still flamed in her. Fletcher's touch scorched her, branded her with the heat that time and distance had never cooled. This time was his love as real and lasting as his passion?

We end the month with **THE PRINCE AND THE PATRIOT**, LOVESWEPT #239, a terrific book from Kathleen Creighton, a favorite LOVESWEPT author. This Valentine features a prince, some crown jewels, a European dynasty and a wonderful happy-ever-after ending. Our heroine, Willa Caris, is not a princess but a patriot. She's committed to protect the crown jewels of Brasovia, the small European country that was her parents' birthplace. Nicholas Francia is a prince in hiding and Willa doesn't know the truth behind his playboy facade. Carried away by tempestuous desire, Nicholas and Willa surrender to their intense attraction and need for one another . . . believing that the goals in their "real" lives are at odds. When the surprising truth is revealed, their love for each other proves to be as strong as their love for their traditions.

Remember to look for the six Valentine covers and spend the month in love—with LOVESWEPT!

Sincerely,

Kate Hartson

Kate Hartson
  Editor
LOVESWEPT
Bantam Books, Inc.
666 Fifth Avenue
New York, NY 10103

The first Delaney trilogy

Heirs to a great dynasty, the Delaney brothers were united by blood, united by devotion to their rugged land . . . and known far and wide as

THE SHAMROCK TRINITY

Bantam's bestselling LOVESWEPT romance line built its reputation on quality and innovation. Now, a remarkable and unique event in romance publishing comes from the same source: THE SHAMROCK TRINITY, three daringly original novels written by three of the most successful women's romance writers today. Kay Hooper, Iris Johansen, and Fayrene Preston have created a trio of books that are dynamite love stories bursting with strong, fascinating male and female characters, deeply sensual love scenes, the humor for which LOVESWEPT is famous, and a deliciously fresh approach to romance writing.

THE SHAMROCK TRINITY—Burke, York, and Rafe: Powerful men . . . rakes and charmers . . . they needed only love to make their lives complete.

☐ *RAFE, THE MAVERICK by Kay Hooper*

Rafe Delaney was a heartbreaker whose ebony eyes held laughing devils and whose lilting voice could charm any lady—or any horse—until a stallion named Diablo left him in the dust. It took Maggie O'Riley to work her magic on the impossible horse . . . and on his bold owner. Maggie's grace and strength made Rafe yearn to share the raw beauty of his land with her, to teach her the exquisite pleasure of yielding to the heat inside her. Maggie was stirred by Rafe's passion, but would his reputation and her ambition keep their kindred spirits apart?   (21846 • $2.75)

LOVESWEPT

☐ *YORK, THE RENEGADE by Iris Johansen*

Some men were made to fight dragons, Sierra Smith thought when she first met York Delaney. The rebel brother had roamed the world for years before calling the rough mining town of Hell's Bluff home. Now, the spirited young woman who'd penetrated this renegade's paradise had awakened a savage and tender possessiveness in York: something he never expected to find in himself. Sierra had known loneliness and isolation too—enough to realize that York's restlessness had only to do with finding a place to belong. Could she convince him that love was such a place, that the refuge he'd always sought was in her arms?

(21847 • $2.75)

☐ *BURKE, THE KINGPIN by Fayrene Preston*

Cara Winston appeared as a fantasy, racing on horseback to catch the day's last light—her silver hair glistening, her dress the color of the Arizona sunset . . . and Burke Delaney wanted her. She was on his horse, on his land: she would have to belong to him too. But Cara was quicksilver, impossible to hold, a wild creature whose scent was midnight flowers and sweet grass. Burke had always taken what he wanted, by willing it or fighting for it; Cara cherished her freedom and refused to believe his love would last. Could he make her see he'd captured her to have and hold forever?

(21848 • $2.75)

The Delaney Dynasty Lives On!

The Bestselling Creators Of The Shamrock Trinity Bring You Three More Sizzling Novels

The Delaneys of Killaroo

Daring women, dreamers, and doers, they would risk anything for the land they loved and the men who possessed their hearts.